GRIMMS' FAIRY TALES

GRIMM'S
FAIRY TALES

VOLUME TWO

Translated by Edgar Taylor
Illustrated by George Cruikshank

Reproduced in facsimile from the
first English edition

**LONDON
THE SCOLAR PRESS
1977**

Printed and published in Great Britain by
The Scolar Press Ltd, Ilkley, Yorkshire
and 39 Great Russell Street, London WC1

ISBN 0 85967 421 5

GERMAN POPULAR STORIES,

&c.

" And so, Gentle Reader, craving thy kind acceptance, I wish thee as much willingness to the reading as I have been forward in the printing, and so I end—Farewell."

Pref. to " *Valentine and Orson . . . . with new pictures lively expressing the history.*"—1677.

GERMAN POPULAR STORIES,

Translated from the

Kinder und Haus-Märchen,

COLLECTED BY

M. M. GRIMM,

From Oral Tradition.

VOL. II.

G. Cruikshank feet?

JAMES ROBINS & C? LONDON.

AND

JOSEPH ROBINS JUN? & C? DUBLIN.

MDCCCXXVI.

ADVERTISEMENT.

THE success of the first volume of *German Popular Stories*, has encouraged one of the translators to venture on a second. The majority of the Tales will be found to have more of the general character of fairy tales, and less of German peculiarity, than those of the first volume, in preparing which, the whole of MM. Grimm's collection was open for the choice of examples of all classes. Perhaps some readers may not think the worse of the present volume on that account.

Two or three Stories have been taken from other collections, as pointed out in the notes.

The Translator cannot let pass the opportunity of thanking the Editor of the new and highly valuable edition of Warton's *History of English Poetry* for the notice he has been pleased to take of the first portion of this little work in his preface. He must apologize for the present volume having, like the first, too little of a character of research to satisfy the antiquarian reader; but he could not alter his plan without interfering too much with the original design, and the unity of its execution. He is, however, glad to see the

subject in such able hands as those into which
" the Editor's Preface" shows it has fallen.

The Translator once thought of following up these
little volumes with one of selections from the
Neapolitan *Pentamerone;* but perhaps the public has had enough of subjects with which, though
he amuses himself, he may tire his readers.

———

O the happy, happy season,
Ere bright Fancy bent to Reason;
When the spirit of our stories
Fill'd the mind with unseen glories;
Told of creatures of the air,
Spirits, fairies, goblins rare,
Guarding man with tenderest care;
When before the blazing hearth,
Listening to the tale of mirth,
Sons and daughters, mother, sire,
Neighbours all drew round the fire;
Lending open ear and faith
To what some learned gossip saith!
   But the fays and all are gone,
Reason, Reason, reigns alone;
Every grace and charm is fled,
All by dullness banished;
Thus we ponder, slow and sad,
After Truth the world is mad;
Ah! believe me, Error too
Hath its charms, nor small, nor few.

Imitated from Voltaire, *by a friend.*

POPULAR STORIES

THE GOOSE-GIRL.

AN old queen, whose husband had been dead some years, had a beautiful daughter. When she grew up, she was betrothed to a prince who lived a great way off; and as the time drew near for her to be married, she got ready to set off on her journey to his country. Then the queen her mother packed up a great many costly things; jewels, and gold, and silver; trinkets, fine dresses, and in short every thing that became a royal bride; for she loved her child very dearly: and she gave her a waiting-maid to ride with her, and give her into the bridegroom's hands; and each had a horse for the journey. Now the princess's horse was called Falada, and could speak.

When the time came for them to set out, the old queen went into her bed-chamber, and took a little knife, and cut off a lock of her hair, and gave it to her daughter, and said, " Take care of it, dear child; for it is a charm that may be of use to you on the road." Then they took a sorrowful leave of each other, and the princess put the lock of her mother's hair into her bosom, got upon her horse, and set off on her journey to her bridegroom's kingdom. One day, as they were riding along by the side of a brook, the princess began to feel very thirsty, and said to her maid, " Pray get down and fetch me some water in my golden cup out of yonder brook, for I want to drink." " Nay," said the maid, " if you are thirsty, get down yourself, and lie down by the water and drink; I shall not be your waiting-maid any longer." Then she was so thirsty that she got down, and knelt over the little brook, and drank, for she was frightened, and dared not bring out her golden cup; and then she wept, and said, " Alas ! what will become of me?" And the lock of hair answered her, and said,

"Alas! alas! if thy mother knew it,
Sadly, sadly her heart would rue it."

But the princess was very humble and meek, so she said nothing to her maid's ill behaviour, but got upon her horse again.

Then all rode further on their journey, till the day grew so warm, and the sun so scorching, that the bride began to feel very thirsty again; and at last when they came to a river she forgot her maid's rude speech, and said, " Pray get down and fetch me some water to drink in my golden cup." But the maid answered her, and even spoke more haughtily than before, " Drink if you will, but I shall not be your waiting-maid." Then the princess was so thirsty that she got off her horse, and lay down, and held her head over the running stream, and cried, and said, " What will become of me?" And the lock of hair answered her again,

"Alas! alas! if thy mother knew it,
Sadly, sadly her heart would rue it."

And as she leaned down to drink, the lock

of hair fell from her bosom, and floated away
with the water, without her seeing it, she was
so frightened.   But her maid saw it, and was
very glad, for she knew the charm, and saw
that the poor bride would be in her power,
now that she had lost the hair.   So when the
bride had done, and would have got upon
Falada again, the maid said, " I shall ride
upon Falada, and you may have my horse instead:" so she was forced to give up her horse,
and soon afterwards to take off her royal
clothes, and put on her maid's shabby
ones.

At last, as they drew near the end of their
journey, this treacherous servant threatened to
kill her mistress if she ever told any one what
had happened. But Falada saw it all, and marked it well. Then the waiting-maid got upon Falada, and the real bride was set upon the other
horse, and they went on in this way till at last
they came to the royal court. There was great
joy at their coming, and the prince flew to
meet them, and lifted the maid from her horse,
thinking she was the one who was to be his
wife; and she was led up stairs to the royal

chamber, but the true princess was told to stay in the court below.

But the old king happened to be looking out of the window, and saw her in the yard below; and as she looked very pretty, and too delicate for a waiting-maid, he went into the royal chamber to ask the bride who it was she had brought with her, that was thus left standing in the court below. " I brought her with me for the sake of her company on the road," said she; "pray give the girl some work to do, that she may not be idle." The old king could not for some time think of any work for her to do; but at last he said, " I have a lad who takes care of my geese; she may go and help him." Now the name of this lad, that the real bride was to help in watching the king's geese, was Curdken.

Soon after, the false bride said to the prince, " Dear husband, pray do me one piece of kind- ness." " That I will," said the prince. " Then tell one of your slaughterers to cut off the head of the horse I rode upon, for it was very unruly, and plagued me sadly on the road:" but the truth was, she was very much afraid lest Falada should speak, and tell all she had done to the princess. She carried her point, and the faithful Falada was killed : but when the true princess heard of it, she wept, and begged the man to nail up Falada's head against a large dark gate of the city, through which she had to pass every morning and evening, that there she might still see him sometimes. Then the slaughterer said he would do as she wished; and cut off the head, and nailed it fast under the dark gate.

Early the next morning, as she and Curdken went out through the gate, she said sorrowfully,

    "Falada, Falada, there thou art hanging!"
and the head answered,

    "Bride, bride, there thou art ganging!
      Alas ! alas ! if thy mother knew it,
      Sadly, sadly her heart would rue it."

Then they went out of the city, and drove the geese on. And when she came to the meadow, she sat down upon a bank there, and let down her waving locks of hair, which were all of pure silver ; and when Curdken saw it glitter in the sun, he ran up, and would

G. Cruikshank fecit

have pulled some of the locks out; but she
cried,

> " Blow, breezes, blow !
> Let Curdken's hat go !
> Blow, breezes, blow !
> Let him after it go !
> O'er hills, dales, and rocks,
> Away be it whirl'd,
> Till the silvery locks
> Are all comb'd and curl'd ! "

Then there came a wind, so strong that it
blew off Curdken's hat; and away it flew over
the hills, and he after it; till, by the time he
came back, she had done combing and curling her hair, and put it up again safe. Then
he was very angry and sulky, and would not
speak to her at all; but they watched the geese
until it grew dark in the evening, and then
drove them homewards.

The next morning, as they were going
through the dark gate, the poor girl looked
up at Falada's head, and cried,

> " Falada, Falada, there thou art hanging ! "

and it answered,

> " Bride, bride, there thou art ganging !
> Alas ! alas ! if thy mother knew it,
> Sadly, sadly her heart would rue it."

'Then she drove on the geese, and sat down again in the meadow, and began to comb out her hair as before; and Curdken ran up to her, and wanted to take hold of it; but she cried out quickly,

> " Blow, breezes, blow !
>   Let Curdken's hat go !
>   Blow, breezes, blow !
>   Let him after it go !
>   O'er hills, dales, and rocks,
>   Away be it whirl'd,
>   Till the silvery locks
>   Are all comb'd and curl'd ! "

Then the wind came and blew his hat, and off it flew a great way, over the hills and far away, so that he had to run after it; and when he came back, she had done up her hair again, and all was safe. So they watched the geese till it grew dark.

In the evening, after they came home, Curdken went to the old king, and said, " I cannot have that strange girl to help me to keep the geese any longer." " Why?" said the king. " Because she does nothing but tease me all day long." Then the king made him tell him all that had passed. And Curdken said,

" When we go in the morning through the dark gate with our flock of geese, she weeps, and talks with the head of a horse that hangs upon the wall, and says,

' Falada, Falada, there thou art hanging ! '

and the head answers,

' Bride, bride, there thou art ganging !
Alas ! alas ! if thy mother knew it,
Sadly, sadly her heart would rue it.' "

And Curdken went on telling the king what had happened upon the meadow where the geese fed; and how his hat was blown away, and he was forced to run after it, and leave his flock. But the old king told him to go out again as usual the next day : and when morning came, he placed himself behind the dark gate, and heard how she spoke to Falada, and how Falada answered ; and then he went into the field, and hid himself in a bush by the meadow's side, and soon saw with his own eyes how they drove the flock of geese, and how, after a little time, she let down her hair that glittered in the sun; and then he heard her say,

" Blow, breezes, blow !
   Let Curdken's hat go !
   Blow, breezes, blow !
   Let him after it go !
   O'er hills, dales, and rocks,
   Away be it whirl'd,
   Till the silvery locks
   Are all comb'd and curl'd ! "

And soon came a gale of wind, and carried
away Curdken's hat, while the girl went on
combing and curling her hair.   All this the
old king saw: so he went home without being
seen ; and when the little goose-girl came
back in the evening, he called her aside, and
asked her why she did so : but she burst into
tears, and said, " That I must not tell you or
any man, or I shall lose my life."

But the old king begged so hard, that she
had no peace till she had told him all, word
for word : and it was very lucky for her that
she did so, for the king ordered royal clothes
to be put upon her, and gazed on her with
wonder, she was so beautiful.   Then he called
his son, and told him, that he had only the
false bride, for that she was merely a waiting-
maid, while the true one stood by.   And the

young king rejoiced when he saw her beauty, and heard how meek and patient she had been ; and, without saying any thing, ordered a great feast to be got ready for all his court. The bridegroom sat at the top, with the false princess on one side, and the true one on the other ; but nobody knew her, for she was quite dazzling to their eyes, and was not at all like the little goose-girl, now that she had her brilliant dress.

When they had eaten and drank, and were very merry, the old king told all the story, as one that he had once heard of, and asked the true waiting-maid what she thought ought to be done to any one who would behave thus. " Nothing better," said this false bride, "than that she should be thrown into a cask stuck round with sharp nails, and that two white horses should be put to it, and should drag it from street to street till she is dead." " Thou art she !" said the old king, " and since thou hast judged thyself, it shall be so done to thee." And the young king was married to his true wife, and they reigned over the kingdom in peace and happiness all their lives.

FAITHFUL JOHN.

An old king fell sick; and when he found his end drawing near, he said, " Let Faithful John come to me." Now Faithful John was the servant that he was fondest of, and was so called because he had been true to his master all his life long. Then when he came to the bed-side, the king said, " My faithful John, I feel that my end draws nigh, and I have now no cares save for my son, who is still young, and stands in need of good counsel. I have no friend to leave him but you; if you do not pledge yourself to teach him all he should know, and to be a father to him, I shall not shut my eyes in peace." Then John said, " I will never leave him, but will serve him faithfully, even though it should cost me my life." And the king said, " I shall now die in peace: after my death, show him the whole palace; all the rooms and vaults, and all the treasures and stores which lie there: but take care how you show him one room,—I mean the one where hangs the picture of the daughter of the king of the golden roof. If he sees it, he will fall deeply in love with her, and will then be plunged into great dangers on her account: guard him in this peril." And when Faithful John had once more pledged his word to the old king, he laid his head on his pillow, and died in peace.

Now when the old king had been carried to his grave, Faithful John told the young king what had passed upon his death-bed, and said, " I will keep my word truly, and be faithful to you as I was always to your father, though it should cost me my life." And the young king wept, and said, " Neither will I ever forget your faithfulness."

The days of mourning passed away, and then Faithful John said to his master, " It is now time that you should see your heritage; I will show you your father's palace." Then he led him about every where, up and down, and let him see all the riches and all the costly rooms; only one room, where the picture stood, he did not open. Now the picture was so placed, that the moment the door opened, you could see it; and it was so beautifully done, that one would think it breathed and had life, and that there was nothing more lovely in the whole world. When the young king saw that Faithful John always went by this door, he said, " Why do you not open that room ? "   " There is something inside," he answered, "which would frighten you." But the king said, " I have seen the whole palace, and I must also know what is in there;" and he went and began to force open the door : but Faithful John held him back, and said, " I gave my word to your father before his death, that I would take heed how I showed you what stands in that room, lest it should lead you and me into great trouble." "The greatest trouble to me," said the young king, will be not to go in and see the room ; I shall have no peace by day or by night until I do; so I shall not go hence until you open it."

Then Faithful John saw that with all he could do or say the young king would have his way; so, with a heavy heart and many foreboding sighs, he sought for the key out of his great bunch; and he opened the door of the room, and entered in first, so as to stand between the king and the picture, hoping he might not see it: but he raised himself upon tiptoes, and looked over John's shoulders; and as soon as he saw the likeness of the lady, so beautiful and shining with gold, he fell down upon the floor senseless. Then Faithful John lifted him up in his arms, and carried him to his bed, and was full of care, and thought to himself, " This trouble has come upon us; O Heaven! what will come of it?"

At last the king came to himself again; but the first thing that he said was, " Whose is that beautiful picture?" " It is the picture of the daughter of the king of the golden roof," said Faithful John. But the king went on, saying, " My love towards her is so great, that if all the leaves on the trees were tongues, they could not speak it; I care not to risk my life to win her; you are my faithful friend, you must aid me."

Then John thought for a long time what was now to be done; and at length said to the king, " All that she has about her is of gold: the tables, stools, cups, dishes, and all the things in her house are of gold; and she

is always seeking new treasures. Now in your
stores there is much gold; let it be worked
up into every kind of vessel, and into all sorts
of birds, wild beasts, and wonderful animals;
then we will take it, and try our fortune." So
the king ordered all the goldsmiths to be
sought for; and they worked day and night,
until at last the most beautiful things were
made: and Faithful John had a ship loaded
with them, and put on a merchant's dress, and
the king did the same, that they might not
be known.

When all was ready, they put out to sea,
and sailed till they came to the coast of the
land where the king of the golden roof reigned.
Faithful John told the king to stay in the
ship, and wait for him; "for perhaps," said
he, "I may be able to bring away the king's
daughter with me: therefore take care that
every thing be in order; let the golden vessels
and ornaments be brought forth, and the whole
ship be decked out with them." And he chose
out something of each of the golden things to
put into his basket, and got ashore, and went
towards the king's palace. And when he came

to the castle yard, there stood by the well side a beautiful maiden, who had two golden pails in her hand, drawing water. And as she drew up the water, which was glittering with gold, she turned herself round, and saw the stranger, and asked him who he was. Then he drew near, and said, " I am a merchant," and opened his basket, and let her look into it; and she cried out, " Oh ! what beautiful things !" and set down her pails, and looked at one after the other. Then she said, " The king's daughter must see all these ; she is so fond of such things, that she will buy all of you." So she took him by the hand, and led him in; for she was one of the waiting-maids of the daughter of the king.

When the princess saw the wares, she was greatly pleased, and said, " They are so beautiful that I will buy them all." But Faithful John said, " I am only the servant of a rich merchant; what I have here is nothing to what he has lying in yonder ship : there he has the finest and most costly things that ever were made in gold." The princess wanted to have them all brought ashore; but he said, " That

would take up many days, there are such a
number; and more rooms would be wanted to
place them in than there are in the greatest
house." But her wish to see them grew still
greater, and at last she said, " Take me to the
ship, I will go myself, and look at your master's wares."

Then Faithful John led her joyfully to
the ship, and the king, when he saw her,
thought that his heart would leap out of his
breast; and it was with the greatest trouble
that he kept himself still. So she got into
the ship, and the king led her down; but
Faithful John staid behind with the steers-
man, and ordered the ship to put off: "Spread
all your sail," cried he, "that she may fly
over the waves like a bird through the
air."

And the king showed the princess the golden
wares, each one singly; the dishes, cups, ba-
sons, and the wild and wonderful beasts; so
that many hours flew away, and she looked
at every thing with delight, and was not aware
that the ship was sailing away. And after she
had looked at the last, she thanked the mer-

chant, and said she would go home; but when she came upon the deck, she saw that the ship was sailing far away from land upon the deep sea, and that it flew along at full sail. "Alas!" she cried out in her fright, "I am betrayed; I am carried off, and have fallen into the power of a roving trader; I would sooner have died." But then the king took her by the hand, and said, "I am not a merchant, I am a king, and of as noble birth as you. I have taken you away by stealth, but I did so because of the very great love I have for you; for the first time that I saw your face, I fell on the ground in a swoon." When the daughter of the king of the golden roof heard all, she was comforted, and her heart soon turned towards him, and she was willing to become his wife.

But it so happened, that whilst they were sailing on the deep sea, Faithful John, as he sat on the prow of the ship playing on his flute, saw three ravens flying in the air towards him. Then he left off playing, and listened to what they said to each other, for he understood their tongue. The first said,

" There he goes! he is bearing away the daughter of the king of the golden roof; let him go!" "Nay," said the second, "there he goes, but he has not got her yet." And the third said, "There he goes; he surely has her, for she is sitting by his side in the ship." Then the first began again, and cried out, "What boots it to him? See you not that when they come to land, a horse of a foxy-red colour will spring towards him; and then he will try to get upon it, and if he does, it will spring away with him into the air, so that he will never see his love again." "True! true!" said the second, "but is there no help?" "Oh! yes, yes!" said the first; "if he who sits upon the horse takes the dagger which is stuck in the saddle and strikes him dead, the young king is saved: but who knows that? and who will tell him, that he who thus saves the king's life will turn to stone from the toes of his feet to his knee?" Then the second said, "True! true! but I know more still; though the horse be dead, the king loses his bride: when they go together into the palace, there lies the bridal dress on the couch, and looks as if it were woven of gold and silver, but it is all brimstone and pitch; and if he puts it on, it will burn him, marrow and bones." "Alas! alas! is there no help?" said the third. "Oh! yes, yes!" said the second, "if some one draws near and throws it into the fire, the young king will be saved. But what boots that? who knows and will tell him, that, if he does, his body from the knee to the heart will be turned to stone?" "More! more! I know more," said the third : "were the dress burnt, still the king loses his bride. After the wedding, when the dance begins, and the young queen dances on, she will turn pale, and fall as though she were dead; and if some one does not draw near and lift her up, and take from her right breast three drops of blood, she will surely die. But if any one knew this, he would tell him, that if he does do so, his body will turn to stone, from the crown of his head to the tip of his toe."

Then the ravens flapped their wings, and flew on; but Faithful John, who had understood it all, from that time was sorrowful, and did not tell his master what he had heard;

for he saw that if he told him, he must himself lay down his life to save him: at last he said to himself, "I will be faithful to my word, and save my master, if it costs me my life."

Now when they came to land, it happened just as the ravens had foretold; for there sprung out a fine foxy-red horse. "See," said the king, "he shall bear me to my palace:" and he tried to mount, but Faithful John leaped before him, and swung himself quickly upon it, drew the dagger, and smote the horse dead. Then the other servants of the king, who were jealous of Faithful John, cried out, "What a shame to kill the fine beast that was to take the king to his palace!" But the king said, "Let him alone, it is my Faithful John; who knows but he did it for some good end?"

Then they went on to the castle, and there stood a couch in one room, and a fine dress lay upon it, that shone with gold and silver; and the young king went up to it to take hold of it, but Faithful John cast it in the fire, and burnt it. And the other servants began again to grumble, and said, "See, now he is burning the wedding dress." But the king said, "Who knows what he does it for? let him alone! he is my faithful servant John."

Then the wedding feast was held, and the dance began, and the bride also came in; but Faithful John took good heed, and looked in her face; and on a sudden she turned pale, and fell as though she were dead upon the ground. But he sprung towards her quickly, lifted her up, and took her and laid her upon a couch, and drew three drops of blood from her right breast. And she breathed again, and came to herself. But the young king had seen all, and did not know why Faithful John had done it; so he was angry at his boldness, and said, "Throw him into prison."

The next morning Faithful John was led forth, and stood upon the gallows, and said, "May I speak out before I die?" and when the king answered "It shall be granted thee," he said, "I am wrongly judged, for I have always been faithful and true:" and then he told what he had heard the ravens say upon the sea, and how he meant to save his master, and had therefore done all these things.

When he had told all, the king called out, "O my most faithful John! pardon! pardon! take him down!" But Faithful John had fallen down lifeless at the last word he spoke, and lay as a stone: and the king and the queen mourned over him; and the king said, "Oh, how ill have I rewarded thy truth!" And he ordered the stone figure to be taken up, and placed in his own room near to his bed; and as often as he looked at it he wept, and said, "O that I could bring thee back to life again, my Faithful John!"

After a time, the queen had two little sons, who grew up, and were her great joy. One day, when she was at church, the two children staid with their father; and as they played about, he looked at the stone figure, and sighed, and cried out, "O that I could bring thee back to life, my Faithful John!" Then the stone began to speak, and said, "O king! thou canst bring me back to life if thou wilt give up for my sake what is dearest to thee." But the king said, "All that I have in the world would I give up for thee." "Then," said the stone, "cut off the heads of thy chil-

dren, sprinkle their blood over me, and I shall
live again." Then the king was greatly shocked : but he thought how Faithful John had
died for his sake, and because of his great truth
towards him ; and rose up and drew his sword
to cut off his children's heads and sprinkle the
stone with their blood; but the moment he
drew his sword Faithful John was alive again,
and stood before his face, and said, "Your
truth is rewarded." And the children sprang
about and played as if nothing had happened.

Then the king was full of joy: and when he
saw the queen coming, to try her, he put
Faithful John and the two children in a large
closet; and when she came in he said to
her, "Have you been at church ?" "Yes,"
said she, "but I could not help thinking
of Faithful John, who was so true to us."
"Dear wife," said the king, "we can bring
him back to life again, but it will cost us both
our little sons, and we must give them up for
his sake." When the queen heard this, she
turned pale and was frightened in her heart;
but she said, "Let it be so; we owe him all,
for his great faith and truth." Then he re-

joiced because she thought as he had thought, and went in and opened the closet, and brought out the children and Faithful John, and said, "Heaven be praised! he is ours again, and we have our sons safe too." So he told her the whole story; and all lived happily together the rest of their lives.

***

THE BLUE LIGHT.

A SOLDIER had served a king his master many years, till at last he was turned off without pay or reward. How he should get his living he did not know: so he set out and journeyed homeward all day in a very downcast mood, until in the evening he came to the edge of a deep wood. The road leading that way, he pushed forward, but had not gone far before he saw a light glimmering through the trees, towards which he bent his weary steps; and soon came to a hut where no one lived but an old witch. The poor fellow begged for a night's lodging and something to eat and drink; but she would listen to nothing : however, he was not easily got rid of; and at last she said, " I think I will take pity on you this once; but if I do, you must dig over all my garden for me in the morning." The soldier agreed very willingly to any thing she asked, and he became her guest.

The next day he kept his word and dug the garden very neatly. The job lasted all day ; and in the evening, when his mistress would have sent him away, he said, " I am so tired with my work that I must beg you to let me stay over the night." The old lady vowed at first she would not do any such thing ; but after a great deal of talk he carried his point, agreeing to chop up a whole cart-load of wood for her the next day.

This task too was duly ended ; but not till towards night ; and then he found himself so tired, that he begged a third night's rest : and this too was given, but only on his pledging his word that he next day would fetch the witch the blue light that burnt at the bottom of the well.

When morning came she led him to the

well's mouth, tied him to a long rope, and let him down. At the bottom sure enough he found the blue light as the witch had said, and at once made the signal for her to draw him up again. But when she had pulled him up so near to the top that she could reach him with her hands, she said, " Give me the light, I will take care of it,"—meaning to play him a trick, by taking it for herself and letting him fall again to the bottom of the well. But the soldier saw through her wicked thoughts, and said, " No, I shall not give you the light till I find myself safe and sound out of the well." At this she became very angry, and dashed him, with the light she had longed for many a year, down to the bottom. And there lay the poor soldier for a while in despair, on the damp mud below, and feared that his end was nigh. But his pipe happened to be in his pocket still half full, and he thought to himself, " I may as well make an end of smoking you out; it is the last pleasure I shall have in this world." So he lit it at the blue light, and began to smoke.

Up rose a cloud of smoke, and on a sud-

den a little black dwarf was seen making his
way through the midst of it, " What do you
want with me, soldier?" said he. " I have no
business with you," answered he. But the
dwarf said, " I am bound to serve you in
every thing, as lord and master of the blue
light." " Then first of all be so good as to
help me out of this well." No sooner said
than done: the dwarf took him by the hand
and drew him up, and the blue light of course
with him. " Now do me another piece of
kindness," said the soldier : " pray let that
old lady take my place in the well." When
the dwarf had done this, and lodged the witch
safely at the bottom, they began to ransack
her treasures; and the soldier made bold to
carry off as much of her gold and silver as
he well could. Then the dwarf said, " If you
should chance at any time to want me, you
have nothing to do but to light your pipe at
the blue light, and I will soon be with you."

The soldier was not a little pleased at his
good luck, and went to the best inn in the
first town he came to, and ordered some fine
clothes to be made, and a handsome room to

be got ready for him.   When all was ready,
he called his little man to him, and said,
" The king sent me away pennyless, and left
me to hunger and want: I have a mind to
show him that it is my turn to be master now;
so bring me his daughter here this evening,
that she may wait upon me, and do what I
bid her."   " That is rather a dangerous
task," said the dwarf. But away he went, took
the princess out of her bed, fast asleep as she
was, and brought her to the soldier.

Very early in the morning he carried her
back : and as soon as she saw her father, she
said, " I had a strange dream last night: I
thought I was carried away through the air to
a soldier's house, and there I waited upon
him as his servant."   Then the king wondered greatly at such a story ; but told her to
make a hole in her pocket and fill it with peas,
so that if it were really as she said, and the
whole was not a dream, the peas might fall
out in the streets as she passed through, and
leave a clue to tell whither she had been taken.
She did so; but the dwarf had heard the king's
plot ; and when evening came, and the soldier

said he must bring him the princess again, he strewed peas over several of the streets, so that the few that fell from her pocket were not known from the others; and the people amused themselves all the next day picking up peas, and wondering where so many came from.

When the princess told her father what had happened to her the second time, he said, " Take one of your shoes with you, and hide it in the room you are taken to." The dwarf heard this also; and when the soldier told him to bring the king's daughter again, he said, " I cannot save you this time; it will be an unlucky thing for you if you are found out—as I think you will." But the soldier would have his own way. " Then you must take care and make the best of your way out of the city gate very early in the morning," said the dwarf. The princess kept one shoe on as her father bid her, and hid it in the soldier's room: and when she got back to her father, he ordered it to be sought for all over the town; and at last it was found where she had hid it. The soldier had run away, it is true; but he had been too slow, and was soon caught and thrown into a strong prison, and loaded with chains :—what was worse, in the hurry of his flight, he had left behind him his great treasure the blue light and all his gold, and had nothing left in his pocket but one poor ducat.

As he was standing very sorrowful at the prison grating, he saw one of his comrades, and calling out to him said, "If you will bring me a little bundle I left in the inn, I will give you a ducat." His comrade thought this very good pay for such a job: so he went away, and soon came back bringing the blue light and the gold. Then the prisoner soon lit his pipe: up rose the smoke, and with it came his old friend the little dwarf. "Do not fear, master," said he: "keep up your heart at your trial, and leave every thing to take its course;—only mind to take the blue light with you." The trial soon came on; the matter was sifted to the bottom; the prisoner found guilty, and his doom passed :—he was ordered to be hung forthwith on the gallows-tree.

But as he was led out, he said he had one
favour to beg of the king. "What is it?"
said his majesty. "That you will deign to
let me smoke one pipe on the road." "Two,
if you like," said the king. Then he lit his
pipe at the blue light, and the black dwarf
was before him in a moment. "Be so good
as to kill, slay, or put to flight all these people," said the soldier: "and as for the king,
you may cut him into three pieces." Then
the dwarf began to lay about him, and soon
got rid of the crowd around: but the king
begged hard for mercy; and, to save his life,
agreed to let the soldier have the princess for
his wife, and to leave the kingdom to him
when he died.

ASHPUTTEL.

THE wife of a rich man fell sick: and when
she felt that her end drew nigh, she called her
only daughter to her bed-side, and said,
"Always be a good girl, and I will look

down from heaven and watch over you."
Soon afterwards she shut her eyes and died,
and was buried in the garden; and the little
girl went every day to her grave and wept,
and was always good and kind to all about
her.   And the snow spread a beautiful white
covering over the grave ; but by the time the
sun had melted it away again, her father had
married another wife.   This new wife had
two daughters of her own, that she brought
home with her : they were fair in face, but
foul at heart, and it was now a sorry time for
the poor little girl.   " What does the good-
for-nothing thing want in the parlour ?" said
they ; " they who would eat bread should
first earn it; away with the kitchen maid !"
Then they took away her fine clothes, and
gave her an old gray frock to put on, and
laughed at her and turned her into the
kitchen.

There she was forced to do hard work; to
rise early before day-light, to bring the water,
to make the fire, to cook and to wash.   Besides that, the sisters plagued her in all sorts
of ways and laughed at her.   In the evening

when she was tired she had no bed to lie
down on, but was made to lie by the hearth
among the ashes; and then, as she was of
course always dusty and dirty, they called
her Ashputtel.

It happened once that the father was going
to the fair, and asked his wife's daughters
what he should bring them. " Fine clothes,"
said the first: " Pearls and diamonds," cried
the second. " Now, child," said he to
his own daughter, " what will you have ? "
" The first sprig, dear father, that rubs
against your hat on your way home," said
she. Then he bought for the two first the
fine clothes and pearls and diamonds they
had asked for: and on his way home as he
rode through a green copse, a sprig of hazle
brushed against him, and almost pushed off
his hat: so he broke it off and brought it
away; and when he got home he gave it to
his daughter. Then she took it and went to
her mother's grave and planted it there, and
cried so much that it was watered with her
tears ; and there it grew and became a fine
tree. Three times every day she went to it

and wept; and soon a little bird came and built its nest upon the tree, and talked with her, and watched over her, and brought her whatever she wished for.

Now it happened that the king of the land held a feast which was to last three days, and out of those who came to it his son was to choose a bride for himself: and Ashputtel's two sisters were asked to come. So they called her up, and said, "Now, comb our hair, brush our shoes, and tie our sashes for us, for we are going to dance at the king's feast." Then she did as she was told, but when all was done she could not help crying, for she thought to herself, she should have liked to go to the dance too; and at last she begged her mother very hard to let her go. "You! Ashputtel?" said she; "you who have nothing to wear, no clothes at all, and who cannot even dance— you want to go to the ball?" And when she kept on begging,—to get rid of her, she said at last, "I will throw this bason-full of peas into the ash heap, and if you have picked them all out in two hours time you shall go to the feast too." Then she threw the peas into

the ashes: but the little maiden ran out at the
back door into the garden, and cried out—

> " Hither, hither, through the sky,
> Turtle-doves and linnets, fly !
> Blackbird, thrush, and chaffinch gay,
> Hither, hither, haste away !
> One and all, come help me quick,
> Haste ye, haste ye,—pick, pick, pick ! "

Then first came two white doves flying in
at the kitchen window; and next came two
turtle-doves; and after them all the little
birds under heaven came chirping and fluttering in, and flew down into the ashes : and
the little doves stooped their heads down and
set to work, pick, pick, pick; and then the
others began to pick, pick, pick ; and picked
out all the good grain and put it in a dish,
and left the ashes. At the end of one hour
the work was done, and all flew out again at
the windows. Then she brought the dish to
her mother, overjoyed at the thought that now
she should go to the wedding. But she said,
" No, no ! you slut, you have no clothes and
cannot dance, you shall not go." And when
Ashputtel begged very hard to go, she said,

" If you can in one hour's time pick two of those dishes of peas out of the ashes, you shall go too." And thus she thought she should at last get rid of her. So she shook two dishes of peas into the ashes; but the little maiden went out into the garden at the back of the house, and cried out as before—

" Hither, hither, through the sky,
   Turtle-doves and linnets, fly !
   Blackbird, thrush, and chaffinch gay,
   Hither, hither, haste away !
   One and all, come help me quick,
   Haste ye, haste ye,—pick, pick, pick !"

Then first came two white doves in at the kitchen window; and next came the turtle-doves; and after them all the little birds under heaven came chirping and hopping about, and flew down about the ashes : and the little doves put their heads down and set to work, pick, pick, pick; and then the others began pick, pick, pick; and they put all the good grain into the dishes, and left all the ashes. Before half an hour's time all was done, and out they flew again. And then Ashputtel took the dishes to her mother, rejoicing to think that she should now go to the ball. But her mother said, " It is all of no use, you cannot go; you have no clothes, and cannot dance, and you would only put us to shame:" and off she went with her two daughters to the feast.

Now when all were gone, and nobody left at home, Ashputtel went sorrowfully and sat down under the hazle-tree, and cried out—

> " Shake, shake, hazle-tree,
> Gold and silver over me !"

Then her friend the bird flew out of the tree and brought a gold and silver dress for her, and slippers of spangled silk : and she put them on, and followed her sisters to the feast. But they did not know her, and thought it must be some strange princess, she looked so fine and beautiful in her rich clothes: and they never once thought of Ashputtel, but took for granted that she was safe at home in the dirt.

The king's son soon came up to her, and took her by the hand and danced with her and no one else: and he never left her hand:

but when any one else came to ask her to dance, he said, " This lady is dancing with me." Thus they danced till a late hour of the night; and then she wanted to go home: and the king's son said, " I shall go and take care of you to your home;" for he wanted to see where the beautiful maid lived. But she slipped away from him unawares, and ran off towards home, and the prince followed her; but she jumped up into the pigeon-house and shut the door. Then he waited till her father came home, and told him that the unknown maiden who had been at the feast had hid herself in the pigeon-house. But when they had broken open the door they found no one within; and as they came back into the house, Ashputtel lay, as she always did, in her dirty frock by the ashes, and her dim little lamp burnt in the chimney: for she had run as quickly as she could through the pigeon-house and on to the hazle-tree, and had there taken off her beautiful clothes, and laid them beneath the tree, that the bird might carry them away, and had seated herself amid the ashes again in her little gray frock.

The next day when the feast was again held, and her father, mother, and sisters were gone, Ashputtel went to the hazle-tree, and said—

"Shake, shake, hazle tree,
Gold and silver over me!"

And the bird came and brought a still finer dress than the one she had worn the day before. And when she came in it to the ball, every one wondered at her beauty: but the king's son, who was waiting for her, took her by the hand, and danced with her; and when any one asked her to dance, he said as before, "This lady is dancing with me." When night came she wanted to go home; and the king's son followed her as before, that he might see into what house she went: but she sprung away from him all at once into the garden behind her father's house. In this garden stood a fine large pear-tree full of ripe fruit; and Ashputtel not knowing where to hide herself jumped up into it without being seen. Then the king's son could not find out where she was gone, but waited till her father came home, and said to him,

" The unknown lady who danced with me has slipt away, and I think she must have sprung into the pear-tree." The father thought to himself, " Can it be Ashputtel ?" So he ordered an axe to be brought; and they cut down the tree, but found no one upon it. And when they came back into the kitchen, there lay Ashputtel in the ashes as usual; for she had slipped down on the other side of the tree, and carried her beautiful clothes back to the bird at the hazle-tree, and then put on her little gray frock.

The third day, when her father and mother and sisters were gone, she went again into the garden, and said—

> " Shake, shake, hazle-tree,
> Gold and silver over me."

Then her kind friend the bird brought a dress still finer than the former one, and slippers which were all of gold : so that when she came to the feast no one knew what to say for wonder at her beauty : and the king's son danced with her alone; and when any one else asked her to dance, he said, " This lady is my partner." Now when night came she wanted to go home; and the king's son would go with her, and said to himself, " I will not lose her this time; " but however she managed to slip away from him, though in such a hurry that she dropped her left golden slipper upon the stairs.

So the prince took the shoe, and went the next day to the king his father, and said, " I will take for my wife the lady that this golden slipper fits." Then both the sisters were overjoyed to hear this; for they had beautiful feet, and had no doubt that they could wear the golden slipper. The eldest went first into the room where the slipper was and wanted to try it on, and the mother stood by. But her great toe could not go into it, and the shoe was altogether much too small for her. Then the mother gave her a knife, and said, " Never mind, cut it off; when you are queen you will not care about toes, you will not want to go on foot." So the silly girl cut her great toe off, and squeezed the shoe on, and went to the king's son. Then

he took her for his bride, and set her beside
him on his horse and rode away with her.

But in their way home they had to pass by
the hazle-tree that Ashputtel had planted,
and there sat a little dove on the branch
singing—

" Back again ! back again ! look to the shoe !
  The shoe is too small, and not made for you!
  Prince ! prince ! look again for thy bride,
  For she 's not the true one that sits by thy side."

Then the prince got down and looked at
her foot, and saw by the blood that streamed
from it what a trick she had played him. So
he turned his horse round and brought the
false bride back to her home, and said, " This
is not the right bride; let the other sister try
and put on the slipper." Then she went into
the room and got her foot into the shoe, all
but the heel, which was too large. But her
mother squeezed it in till the blood came, and
took her to the king's son ; and he set her as
his bride by his side on his horse, and rode
away with her.

But when they came to the hazle-tree the little dove sate there still, and sang—

" Back again ! back again ! look to the shoe !
The shoe is too small, and not made for you !
Prince ! prince ! look again for thy bride,
For she 's not the true one that sits by thy side."

Then he looked down and saw that the blood streamed so from the shoe that her white stockings were quite red. So he turned his horse and brought her back again also. " This is not the true bride," said he to the father; " have you no other daughters ? " "No," said he; " there is only a little dirty Ashputtel here, the child of my first wife; I am sure she cannot be the bride." However, the prince told him to send her. But the mother said " No, no, she is much too dirty, she will not dare to show herself:" however, the prince would have her come. And she first washed her face and hands, and then went in and curtsied to him, and he reached her the golden slipper. Then she took her clumsy shoe off her left foot, and put on the golden slipper ; and it fitted her as if it had been made for her. And when he drew near and looked at her face he knew her, and said, " This is the right bride." But the mother and both the sisters were frightened and turned pale with anger as he took Ashputtel on his horse, and rode away with her. And when they came to the hazle-tree, the white dove sang—

" Home ! home ! look at the shoe !
  Princess ! the shoe was made for you !
  Prince ! prince ! take home thy bride,
  For she is the true one that sits by thy side ! "

And when the dove had done its song, it came flying and perched upon her right shoulder, and so went home with her.

THE YOUNG GIANT AND THE TAILOR.

A HUSBANDMAN had once a son, who was born no bigger than my thumb, and for many years did not grow a hair's breadth taller. One day as the father was going to plough in the field, the little fellow said, " Father, let me go too." " No," said his father ;

Ge.º Cruikshank fecit D.

" stay where you are, you can do no good out of doors, and if you go perhaps I may lose you." Then little Thumbling fell a-crying: and his father, to quiet him, at last said he might go. So he put him in his pocket, and when he was in the field pulled him out and set him upon a newly made furrow, that he might look about. While he was sitting there, a great giant came striding over the hill. " Do you see that tall steeple-man?" said the father: " he will run away with you." (Now he only said this to frighten the little boy if he should be naughty.) But the giant had long legs, and with two or three strides he really came close to the furrow, and picked up little Thumbling to look at him; and taking a liking to the little chap went off with him. The father stood by all the time, but could not say a word for fright; for he thought his child was really lost, and that he should never see him again.

But the giant took care of him at his house in the woods, and laid him in his bosom and fed him with the same food that he lived on himself. So Thumbling, instead of being a little dwarf, became like the giant—tall and stout and strong: so that at the end of two years when the old giant took him into the wood to try him, and said, " Pull up that birch-tree for yourself to walk with;" the lad was so strong that he tore it up by the root. The giant thought he should make him a still stronger man than this: so after taking care of him two years more, he took him into the wood to try his strength again. This time he took hold of one of the thickest oaks, and pulled it up as if it were mere sport to him. Then the old giant said, " Well done, my man, you will do now." So he carried him back to the field where he first found him.

His father happened to be just then ploughing as the young giant went up to him, saying, " Look here, father, see who I am ;—don't you see I am your son ?" But the husbandman was frightened, and cried out, " No, no, you are not my son ; begone about your business." " Indeed, I am your son ; let me plough a little, I can plough as well as you." " No, go your ways," said the father.

but as he was afraid of the tall man, he at
last let go the plough and sat down on the
ground beside it. Then the youth laid hold
of the ploughshare, and though he only pushed with one hand, he drove it deep into the
earth. The ploughman cried out, "If you
must plough, pray do not push so hard;
you are doing more harm than good;" but
he took off the horses, and said, "Father, go
home and tell my mother to get ready a good
dinner; I'll go round the field meanwhile."
So he went on driving the plough without
any horses, till he had done two mornings'
work by himself; then he harrowed it, and
when all was over, took up plough, harrow,
horses and all, and carried them home like a
bundle of straw.

When he reached the house he sat himself
down on the bench, saying, "Now, mother,
is dinner ready?" "Yes," said she, for she
dared not deny him; so she brought two large
dishes full, enough to have lasted herself and
her husband eight days; however, he soon ate
it all up, and said that was but a taste. "I
see very well, father, that I sha'n't get enough

to eat at your house; so if you will give me an iron walking-stick, so strong that I cannot break it against my knees, I will go away again." The husbandman very gladly put his two horses to the cart and drove them to the forge, and brought back a bar of iron as long and as thick as his two horses could draw; but the lad laid it against his knee; and snap! it went like a broken beanstalk. "I see, father," said he, "you can get no stick that will do for me, so I'll go and try my luck by myself."

Then away he went, and turned blacksmith, and travelled till he came to a village where lived a miserly smith, who earned a good deal of money, but kept all he got to himself, and gave nothing away to any body. The first thing he did was to step into the smithy, and ask if the smith did not want a journeyman. "Aye," said the cunning fellow, (as he looked at him and thought what a stout chap he was, and how lustily he would work and earn his bread,) "what wages do you ask?" "I want no pay," said he; "but every fortnight when the other workmen are paid, you shall let me give you two strokes over the shoulders to amuse myself." The old smith thought to himself he could bear this very well, and reckoned on saving a great deal of money; so the bargain was soon struck.

The next morning the new workman was about to begin to work; but at the first stroke that he hit, when his master brought him the iron red hot, he shivered it in pieces, and the anvil sunk so deep into the earth, that he could not get it out again. This made the old fellow very angry; "Halloo!" cried he, " I can't have you for a workman, you are too clumsy; we must put an end to our bargain." " Very well," said the other, "but you must pay for what I have done, so let me give you only one little stroke, and then the bargain is all over." So saying, he gave him a thump that tossed him over a load of hay that stood near. Then he took the thickest bar of iron on the forge for a walking-stick, and went on his way.

When he had journeyed some way, he came to a farm-house, and asked the farmer if he wanted a foreman. The farmer said, " Yes," and the same wages were agreed for as before with the blacksmith. The next morning the workmen were all to go into the wood; but the giant was found to be fast asleep in his bed when the rest were all up and ready to start. "Come, get up," said one of them to him, "it is high time to be stirring; you must go with us." "Go your way," muttered he sulkily, "I shall have done my work and get home long before you." So he lay in bed two hours longer, and at last got up and cooked and ate his breakfast, and then at his leisure harnessed his horses to go to the wood. Just before the wood was a hollow, through which all must pass; so he drove the cart on first, and built up behind him such a mound of faggots and briars that no horse could pass. This done, he drove on, and as he was going into the wood met the others coming out on their road home; "Drive away," said he, "I shall be home before you still." However, he only went a very little way into the wood and tore up one of the largest timber trees, put it into his cart, and turned about homewards. When he came to the pile of faggots, he found all the others standing there, not being able to pass by. " So," said he, "you see if you had staid with me, you would have been home just as soon, and might have slept an hour or two longer." Then he took his tree on one shoulder, and his cart on the other, and pushed through as easily as though he were laden with feathers, and when he reached the yard showed the tree to the farmer, and asked if it was not a famous walking-stick. " Wife," said the farmer, " this man is worth something; if he sleeps longer, still he works better than the rest."

Time rolled on, and he had served the farmer his whole year; so when his fellow-labourers were paid, he said he also had a right to take his wages. But great dread came upon the farmer, at the thought of the blows he was to have, so he begged him to give up the old bargain, and take his whole farm and stock instead. " Not I," said he, " I will be no farmer; I am foreman, and so I mean to keep, and be paid as we agreed." Finding he could do nothing with him, the farmer only begged one fortnight's respite, and called together all his friends, to ask their advice in the matter. They bethought themselves for a long time, and at last agreed that the shortest way was to kill this troublesome foreman. The next thing was to settle how it was to be done; and it was agreed that he should be ordered to carry into the yard some great mill-stones, and to put them on the edge of a well; that then he should be sent down to clean it out, and when he was at the bottom, the mill-stones should be pushed down upon his head. Every thing went right, and when the foreman was safe in the well, the stones were rolled in. As they struck the bottom, the water splashed to the very top. Of course they thought his head must be crashed to pieces; but he only cried out, " Drive away the chickens from the well; they are pecking about in the sand above me, and throwing it into my eyes, so that I cannot see." When his job was done, up he sprung from the well, saying, " Look here ! see what a fine neck-cloth I have!" as he pointed to one of the mill-stones, that had fallen over his head, and hung about his neck.

The farmer was again overcome with fear, and begged another fortnight to think of it. So his friends were called together again, and at last gave this advice; that the foreman should be sent and made to grind corn by night at the haunted mill, whence no man had ever yet come out in the morning alive. That very evening he was told to carry eight bushels of corn to the mill, and grind them in the night. Away he went to the loft, put two bushels in his right pocket, two in his left, and four in a long sack slung over his shoulders, and then set off to the mill. The miller told him he might grind there in the day time, but not by night, for the mill was bewitched, and whoever went in at night had been found dead in the morning: " Never mind, miller, I shall come out safe," said he ; " only make haste and get out of the way, and look out for me in the morning."

So he went into the mill and put the corn into the hopper, and about twelve o'clock sat himself down on the bench in the miller's room. After a little time the door all at once opened of itself, and in came a large table.

On the table stood wine and meat, and many good things besides: all seemed placed there by themselves; at any rate there was no one to be seen. The chairs next moved themselves round it, but still neither guests nor servants came; till all at once he saw fingers handling the knives and forks and putting food on the plates, but still nothing else was to be seen. Now our friend felt somewhat hungry as he looked at the dishes, so he sat himself down at the table and ate whatever he liked best; and when he had had enough, and the plates were empty, on a sudden he heard something blow out the lights. When it was pitch dark he felt a tremendous blow upon his head; "If I get such another box on the ear," said he, "I shall just give it back again;" and this he really did, when the next blow came. Thus the game went on all night; and he never let fear get the better of him, but kept dealing his blows round, till at day-break all was still. "Well, miller," said he in the morning, "I have had some little slaps on the face, but I've given as good, I'll warrant you; and meantime I have eaten as much as I liked." The miller was glad to find the charm was broken, and would have given him a great deal of money; " I want no money, I have quite enough," said he, as he took the meal on his back, and went home to his master to claim his wages.

But the farmer was in a rage, knowing there was no help for him, and paced the room up and down till the drops of sweat ran down his forehead. Then he opened the window for a little fresh air, and before he was aware, his foreman gave him the first blow, and kicked him out of the window over the hills and far away, and next sent his wife after him; and there, for aught I know, they may be flying in the air still: but the young giant took up his iron walking-stick and walked off.

Perhaps this was the same giant that the Bold little Tailor met, when he set out on his travels, as I will tell you next.

It was a fine summer morning when this

little man bound his girdle round his body, and looked about his house to see if there was any thing good to take with him on his journey into the wide world.   He could only find an old cheese; but that was better than nothing; so he took it up; and, as he was going out, the old hen met him at the door, and he packed her too into his wallet with the cheese.   Then off he set, and when he had climbed a high hill, he found the giant sitting on the top. " Good day, comrade," said he; " there you sit at your ease, and look the wide world over : I have a mind to go and try my luck in that same world; what do you say to going with me ? "   Then the giant looked at him, and said, " You are a poor trumpery little knave."   " That may be," said the tailor; " but we shall see who is the best man of the two."   The giant, finding the little man so bold, began to be a little more respectful, and said they would soon try who was master. So he took a large stone in his hand and squeezed it till water dropped from it;   " Do that," said he, " if you have a mind to be thought a strong man."   " Is that all ? " said the tailor; " I will soon do as much ;" so he put his hand in his wallet, pulled out the cheese (which was quite new), and squeezed it till the whey ran out. " What do you say now, Mr. Giant ? my squeeze was a better one than yours." Then the giant, not seeing that it was only a cheese, did not know what to say for himself, though he could hardly believe his eyes ; at last he took up a stone, and threw it up so high that it went almost out of sight ; " Now then, little pygmy, do that if you can." " Very good," said the other ; " your throw was not a bad one, but after all your stone fell to the ground; I will throw something that shall not fall at all." " That you can't do," said the giant : but the tailor took his old hen out of the wallet, and threw her up in the air, and she, pleased enough to be set free, flew away out of sight. "Now, Comrade," said he, " what do you say to that ? " " I say you are a clever hand," said the giant, " but we will now try how you can work."

Then he led him into the wood, where a fine oak tree lay felled. " Now let us drag it out of the wood together." " Very well ;

do you take the thick end, and I will carry all the top and branches, which are much the largest and heaviest." So the giant took the trunk and laid it on his shoulder; but the cunning little rogue, instead of carrying any thing, sat himself at his ease among the branches, and let the giant carry stem, branches, and tailor into the bargain. All the way they went he made merry, and whistled and sang his song as if carrying the tree were mere sport; while the giant after he had borne it a good way could carry it no longer, and said, " I must let it fall." Then the tailor sprung down and held the tree as if he were carrying it, saying, " What a shame that such a big lout as you cannot carry a tree like this!" Then on they went together till they came to a tall cherry tree; and the giant took hold of the top stem, and bent it down to pluck the ripest fruit, and when he had done, gave it over to his friend that he too might eat; but the little man was so weak that he could not hold the tree down, and up he went with it swinging in the air. " Halloo !" said the giant, " what now? can't

-G.Cruikshk.foot-

you hold that twig?" "To be sure I could," said the other; "but don't you see there's a huntsman, who is going to shoot into the bush where we stood? so I took a jump over the tree to be out of his way; do you do the same." The giant tried to follow, but the tree was far too high to jump over, and he only stuck fast in the branches, for the tailor to laugh at him. "Well! you are a fine fellow after all," said the giant; "so come home and sleep with me and a friend of mine in the mountains to-night."

The tailor had no business upon his hands, so he did as he was bid, and the giant gave him a good supper, and a bed to sleep upon; but the tailor was too cunning to lie down upon it, and crept slily into a corner, and slept there soundly. When midnight came, the giant came softly in with his iron walking-stick, and gave such a stroke upon the bed where he thought his guest was lying, that he said to himself, "It's all up now with that grasshopper; I shall have no more of his tricks." In the morning the giants went off into the woods, and quite forgot him, till all on a sudden they met him trudging along, whistling a merry tune ; and so frightened were they at the sight, that they both ran away as fast as they could.

Then on went the little tailor following his spuddy nose, till at last he reached the king's court, and began to brag very loud of his mighty deeds, saying he was come to serve the king. To try him, they told him that the two giants who lived in a part of the kingdom a long way off, were become the dread of the whole land; for they had begun to rob, plunder and ravage all about them, and that if he was so great a man as he said, he should have a hundred soldiers and should set out to fight these giants, and if he beat them he should have half the kingdom. " With all my heart ! " said he; " but as for your hundred soldiers, I believe I shall do as well without them." However, they set off together till they came to a wood : " Wait here, my friends," said he to the soldiers, " I will soon give a good account of these giants :" and on he went casting his sharp little eye here, there, and every where around him. After a

while he spied them both lying under a tree,
and snoring away till the very boughs whistled
with the breeze. " The game's won, for a
penny," said the little man, as he filled his
wallet with stones, and climbed the tree under
which they lay.

As soon as he was safely up, he threw one
stone after another at the nearest giant, till at
last he woke up in a rage, and shook his companion, crying out, " What did you strike me
for ?" " Nonsense ! you are dreaming," said
the other, " I did not strike you." Then
both lay down to sleep again, and the tailor
threw stones at the second giant, till he sprung
up and cried, " What are you about ? you
struck me." " I did not," said the other ; and
on they wrangled for a while, till as both were
tired they made up the matter, and fell asleep
again. But then the tailor began his game once
more, and flung the largest stone he had in his
wallet with all his force and hit the first giant
on the nose. " That is too bad," cried he, as
if he was mad, " I will not bear it." So he
struck the other a mighty blow ; he of course
was not pleased at this, and gave him just

such another box on the ear; and at last a
bloody battle began; up flew the trees by
the roots, the rocks and stones went bang at
one another's heads, and in the end both lay
dead upon the spot. "It is a good thing,"
said the tailor, "that they let my tree stand,
or I must have made a fine jump." Then
down he ran, and took his sword and gave
each of them a very fine wound or two on
the breast and set off to look for the soldiers.
"There 'lie the giants," said he; "I have
killed them, but it has been no small job, for
they even tore trees up in their struggle."
"Have you any wounds?" asked they.
"That is a likely matter, truly," said he;
"they have not touched a hair of my head."
But the soldiers would not believe him till
they rode into the wood and found the giants
weltering in their blood, and the trees lying
around torn up by the roots.

The king, after he had got rid of his ene-
mies, was not much pleased at the thoughts
of giving up half his kingdom to a tailor; so
he said, "You have not yet done; in the palace court lies a bear with whom you must

pass the night, and if when I rise in the morning I find you still living, you shall then have
your reward." Now he thought he had got rid
of him, for the bear had never yet let any one
go away alive who had come within reach of
his claws.   " Very well," said the tailor, " I
am willing."

So when evening came our little tailor
was led out and shut up in the court with the
bear, who rose at once to give him a friendly
welcome with his paw. " Softly, softly, my
friend," said he; " I know a way to please
you;" then at his ease and as if he cared nothing about the matter, he pulled out of his
pocket some fine walnuts, cracked them, and
ate the kernels. When the bear saw this, he
took a great fancy to having some nuts too;
so the tailor felt in his pocket and gave him a
handful, not of walnuts, but nice round pebbles. The bear snapt them up, but could not
crack one of them, do what he would. " What
a clumsy thick head thou art !" thought the
beast to itself; " thou canst not crack a nut
to-day." Then said he to the tailor,
" Friend, pray crack me the nuts."   " Why,

what a lout you are," said the tailor, "to have such a jaw as that, and not to be able to crack a little nut! Well! engage to be friends with me and I 'll help you." So he took the stones, and slily changed them for nuts, put them in his mouth, and crack! they went. " I must try for myself, however," said the bear; " now I see how you do it, I am sure I can do it myself." Then the tailor gave him the cobble stones again, and the bear lay down and worked away as hard as he could, and bit and bit with all his force till he broke all his teeth, and lay down quite tired.

But the tailor began to think this would not last long, and that the bear might find him out and break the bargain; so he pulled a fiddle out from under his coat and played him a tune. As soon as the bear heard it, he could not help jumping up and beginning to dance; and when he had jigged away for a while, the thing pleased him so much that he said, " Hark ye, friend! is the fiddle hard to play upon?" " No! not at all!" said the other; " look ye, I lay my left hand here, and then I take the bow with my right hand thus, and

G. Cruikshank fec.

scrape it over the strings there, and away it goes merrily, hop, sa, sa ! fal, lal, la !" "Will you teach me to fiddle," said the bear, " so that I may have music whenever I want to dance ? " " With all my heart; but let me look at your claws, they are so very long that I must first clip your nails a little bit." Then the bear lifted up his paws one after another, and the tailor screwed them down tight, and said, " Now wait till I come with my scissars." So he left the bear to growl as loud as he liked, and laid himself down on a heap of straw in the corner and slept soundly. In the morning when the king came, he found the tailor sitting merrily eating his breakfast, and could no longer help keeping his word; and thus the little man became a great one.

THE CROWS AND THE SOLDIER.

A worthy soldier had saved a good deal of money out of his pay; for he worked hard, and did not spend all he earned in eating and drinking, as many others do. Now he had two comrades who were great rogues, and wanted to rob him of his money, but behaved outwardly towards him in a friendly way. "Comrade," said they to him one day, "why should we stay here shut up in this town like prisoners, when you at any rate have earned enough to live upon for the rest of your days in peace and plenty at home by your own fireside?" They talked so often to him in this manner, that he at last said he would go and try his luck with them; but they all the time thought of nothing but how they should manage to steal his money from him.

When they had gone a little way, the two rogues said, "We must go by the right hand road, for that will take us quickest into another country where we shall be safe." Now they knew all the while that what they were saying was untrue; and as soon as the soldier said, "No, that will take us straight back into the town we came from; we must keep on the left hand;" they picked a quarrel with him, and said, "What do you give yourself airs for? you know nothing about it:"

and then they fell upon him and knocked him down, and beat him over the head till he was blind. Then they took all the money out of his pockets and dragged him to a gallows tree that stood hard by, bound him fast down at the foot of it, and went back into the town with the money; but the poor blind man did not know where he was ; and he felt all around him, and finding that he was bound to a large beam of wood, thought it was a cross, and said, " After all, they have done kindly in leaving me under a cross ; now Heaven will guard me ;" so he raised himself up and began to pray.

When night came on, he heard something fluttering over his head. It turned out to be three crows, who flew round and round, and at last perched upon the tree. By and by they began to talk together, and he heard one of them say, " Sister, what is the best news with you to-day?" " O, if men knew what we know !" said the other; " the princess is ill, and the king has vowed to marry her to any one who will cure her; but this none can do, for she will not be well until yonder flower is burnt to ashes and swallowed by her." "Oh, indeed," said the other crow, "if men did but know what we know! to-night will fall from heaven a dew of such healing power, that even the blind man who washes his eyes with it will see again;" and the third spoke, and said, "O if men knew what we know! the flower is wanted but for one, the dew is wanted but for few; but there is a great dearth of water in the town; all the wells are dried up; and no one knows that they must take away the large square stone out of the market-place, and dig underneath it, and that then the finest water will spring up."

When the three crows had done talking, he heard them fluttering round again, and at last away they flew. Greatly wondering at what he had heard, and overjoyed at the thoughts of getting his sight, he tried with all his strength to break loose from his bonds; at last he found himself free, and plucked some of the grass that grew beneath him and washed his eyes with the dew that had fallen upon it. At once his eye-sight came to him again, and he saw by the light of the moon and the stars that he was beneath the gallows-tree, and not the cross, as he had thought. Then he gathered together in a bottle as much of the dew as he could to take away with him, and looked around till he saw the flower that grew close by; and when he had burned it he gathered up the ashes, and set out on his way towards the king's court.

When he reached the palace, he told the king he was come to cure the princess; and when she had taken of the ashes and been made well, he claimed her for his wife, as the reward that was to be given; but the king looking upon him and seeing that his clothes were so shabby, would not keep his word, and thought to get rid of him by saying, " Whoever wants to have the princess for his wife, must find enough water for the use of the town, where there is this summer a great dearth." Then the soldier went out and told the people to take up the square stone in the market-place and dig for water underneath; and when they had done so there came up a fine spring, that gave enough water for the whole town. So the king could no longer get off giving him his daughter, and they were married and lived happily together.

Some time after, as he was walking one day through a field, he met his two wicked comrades who had treated him so basely. Though they did not know him, he knew them at once, and went up to them and said, "Look upon me, I am your old comrade whom you beat and robbed and left blind; Heaven has defeated your wicked wishes, and turned all the mischief which you brought upon me into good luck." When they heard this they fell at his feet and begged for pardon, and he had a kind and good heart, so he forgave them, and took them to his palace and gave them food and clothes. And he told them all that had happened to him, and how he had reached these honours. After they had heard the whole story they said to themselves, "Why should not we go and sit some night under the gallows? we may hear something that will bring us good luck too."

Next night they stole away; and, when they had sat under the tree a little while, they heard a fluttering noise over their heads; and the three crows came and perched upon it. "Sisters," said one of them, "some one must have overheard us, for all the world is talking of the wonderful things that have happened: the princess is well; the flower has been plucked and burnt; a blind man's sight has been given him again, and they have dug a fresh well that gives water to the whole town: let us look about, perhaps we may find some one near; if we do he shall rue the day." Then they began to flutter about, and soon found out the two men below, and flew at them in a rage, beating and pecking them in the face with their wings and beaks till they were quite blind, and lay nearly dead upon the ground under the gallows. The next day passed over and they did not return to the palace; and their old comrade began to wonder where they had been, and went out the following morning in search of them, and at last found them where they lay, dreadfully repaid for all their folly and baseness.

PEE-WIT.

A POOR countryman whose name was Pee-wit lived with his wife in a very quiet way in the parish where he was born. One day, as he was ploughing with his two oxen in the field, he heard all on a sudden some one calling out his name. Turning round, he saw nothing but a bird that kept crying Pee-wit! Pee-wit! Now this poor bird is called a Pee-wit, and like the cuckoo always keeps crying out its own name. But the country-man thought it was mocking him, so he took up a huge stone and threw at it; the bird flew off safe and sound, but the stone fell upon the head of one of the oxen, and killed him on the spot. "What is to be done with the odd one?" thought Pee-wit to himself as he looked at the ox that was left; so without more ado he killed him too, skinned them both, and set out for the neighbouring town, to sell the hides to the tanner for as much as he could get. He soon found out where the tanner lived, and knocked at the door. Be-tore, however, the door was opened, he saw through the window that the mistress of the house was hiding in an old chest a friend of hers, whom she seemed to wish no one should see. By and by the door was opened, "What do you want?" said the woman. Then he told her that he wanted to sell his hides; and it came out that the tanner was not at home, and that no one there ever made bargains but himself. The countryman said he would sell cheap, and did not mind giving his hides for the old chest in the corner; meaning the one he had seen the good woman's friend get into. Of course the wife would not agree to this; and they went on talking the matter over so long, that at last in came the tanner and asked what it was all about. Pee-wit told him the whole story, and asked him whether he would give the old chest for the hides. "To be sure I will," said he; and scolded his wife for saying nay to such a bargain, which she ought to have been glad to make if the countryman was willing. Then up he took the chest on his shoulders, and all the good woman could say mattered nothing;

away it went into the countryman's cart, and
off he drove. But when they had gone some
way, the young man within began to make
himself heard, and to beg and pray to be let
out. Pee-wit, however, was not to be brought
over; till at last after a long parley a thousand dollars were bid and taken; the money
was paid, and at that price the poor fellow
was set free, and went about his business.

Then Pee-wit went home very happy, and
built a new house and seemed so rich that his
neighbours wondered, and said, " Pee-wit
must have been where the golden snow falls."
So they took him before the next justice of
the peace, to give an account of himself, and
show that he came honestly by his wealth;
and then he told them that he had sold his
hides for one thousand dollars. When
they heard it they all killed their oxen and
would sell the hides to the same tanner;
but the justice said, " My maid shall have
the first chance;" so off she went, and when
she came to the tanner, he laughed at them
all, and said he had given their neighbour
nothing but an old chest.

At this they were all very angry, and laid their heads together to work him some mischief, which they thought they could do while he was digging in his garden. All this, however, came to the ears of the countryman, who was plagued with a sad scold for his wife; and he thought to himself, "If any one is to come into trouble, I don't see why it should not be my wife, rather than me;" so he said to her that he wished she would humour him in a whim he had taken into his head, and would put on his clothes, and dig the garden in his stead. The wife did what was asked, and next morning began digging; but soon came some of the neighbours, and, thinking it was Pee-wit, threw a stone at her, (harder perhaps than they meant,) and killed her at once. Poor Pee-wit was rather sorry at this, but still thought that he had had a lucky escape for himself, and that perhaps he might after all turn the death of his wife to some account: so he dressed her in her own clothes, put a basket with fine fruit (which was now scarce, it being winter) into her hand, and set her by the road side on a broad bench.

After a while came by a fine coach with six horses, servants, and outriders, and within sat a noble lord who lived not far off. When his lordship saw the beautiful fruit, he sent one of the servants to the woman to ask what was the price of her goods. The man went and asked "What is the price of this fruit?" No answer. He asked again. No answer: and when this had happened three times, he became angry; and, thinking she was asleep, gave her a blow, and down she fell backwards into the pond that was behind the seat. Then up ran Pee-wit, and cried and sorrowed because they had drowned his poor wife, and threatened to have the lord and his servants tried for what they had done. His lordship begged him to be easy, and offered to give him the coach and horses, servants and all; so the countryman after a long time let himself be appeased a little, took what they gave, got into the coach and set off towards his own home again.

As he came near, the neighbours wondered much at the beautiful coach and horses, and still more when they stopped, and Pee-wit got out at his own door. Then he told them the whole story, which only vexed them still more; so they took him and fastened him up in a tub and were going to throw him into the lake that was hard by. Whilst they were rolling the tub on before them towards the water, they passed by an alehouse and stopped to refresh themselves a little before they put an end to Pee-wit; meantime they tied the tub to a tree and there left it while they were enjoying themselves within doors.

Pee-wit no sooner found himself alone than he began to turn over in his mind how he could get free. He listened, and soon heard Ba, ba! from a flock of sheep and lambs that were coming by. Then he lifted up his voice, and shouted out, " I will not be burgo-master, I say; I will not be made burgo-master." The shepherd hearing this went up, and said, " What is all this noise about?" " O!" said Pee-wit, " my neighbours will make me burgomaster against my will; and when I told them I would not agree, they put me into the cask and are going to throw me into the lake." " I should like very well

to be burgomaster if I were you," said the
shepherd. " Open the cask then," said the
other, " and let me out, and get in yourself,
and they will make you burgomaster instead
of me." No sooner said than done, the
shepherd was in, Pee-wit was out; and as
there was nobody to take care of the shepherd's flock, he drove it off merrily towards
his own house.

When the neighbours came out of the
alehouse, they rolled the cask on, and the
shepherd began to cry out, " I *will* be burgomaster now; I *will* be burgomaster now."
" I dare say you will, but you shall take a
swim first," said a neighbour, as he gave the
cask the last push over into the lake. This
done, away they went home merrily, leaving
the shepherd to get out as well as he could.

But as they came in at one side of the village, who should they meet coming in the
other way but Pee-wit driving a fine flock of
sheep and lambs before him. " How came
you here?" cried all with one voice. "O!
the lake is enchanted," said he; " when you
threw me in, I sunk deep and deep into the

water, till at last I came to the bottom; there
I knocked out the bottom of the cask and
found myself in a beautiful meadow with fine
flocks grazing upon it, so I chose a few for
myself, and here I am." " Cannot we have
some too?" said they. " Why not? there are
hundreds and thousands left; you have nothing to do but jump in and fetch them out."

So all agreed they would dive for sheep;
the justice first, then the clerk, then the
constables, and then the rest of the parish,
one after the other. When they came to the
side of the lake, the blue sky was covered with
little white clouds like flocks of sheep, and
all were reflected in the clear water: so they
called out, " There they are, there they are
already;" and fearing lest the justice should
get every thing, they jumped in all at once;
and Pee-wit jogged home, and made himself
happy with what he had got, leaving them to
find their flocks by themselves as well as
they could.

HANS AND HIS WIFE GRETTEL.

I. *Showing who Grettel was.*

THERE was once a little maid named Grettel: she wore shoes with red heels, and when she went abroad she turned out her toes, and was very merry, and thought to herself, "What a pretty girl I am!" And when she came home, to put herself in good spirits, she would tipple down a drop or two of wine; and as wine gives a relish for eating, she would take a taste of every thing when she was cooking, saying, "A cook ought to know whether a thing tastes well." It happened one day that her master said, "Grettel, this evening I have a friend coming to sup with me; get two fine fowls ready." "Very well, sir," said Grettel. Then she killed the fowls, plucked, and trussed them, put them on the spit, and when evening came put them to the fire to roast. The fowls turned round and round, and soon began to look nice and brown, but the guest did not come. Then Grettel cried out, "Master, if the guest does

not come I must take up the fowls, but it will
be a shame and a pity if they are not eaten
while they are hot and good."   " Well,"
said her master, " I 'll run and tell him to
come."   As soon as he had turned his back,
Grettel stopped the spit, and laid it with the
fowls upon it on one side, and thought to herself, " Standing by the fire makes one very tired
and thirsty; who knows how long they will
be ? meanwhile I will just step into the cellar
and take a drop." So off she ran, put down
her pitcher, and said " Your health, Grettel,"
and took a good draught.   " This wine is a
good friend," said she to herself, " it breaks
one's heart to leave it." Then up she trotted,
put the fowls down to the fire, spread some
butter over them, and turned the spit merrily
round again.

The fowls soon smelt so good, that she
thought to herself, " They are very good, but
they may want something still; I had better
taste them and see." So she licked her fingers, and said, " O ! how good ! what a
shame and a pity that they are not eaten ! "
Away she ran to the window to see if her

master and his friend were coming; but nobody was in sight: so she turned to the fowls
again, and thought it would be better for
her to eat a wing than that it should be
burnt. So she cut one wing off, and ate it, and
it tasted very well; and as the other was quite
done enough, she thought it had better be
cut off too, or else her master would see one
was wanting. When the two wings were
gone, she went again to look out for her master, but could not see him. " Ah ! " thought
she to herself, " who knows whether they will
come at all ? very likely they have turned into
some tavern: O Grettel ! Grettel ! make
yourself happy, take another draught, and
eat the rest of the fowl; it looks so oddly as
it is; when you have eaten all, you will be
easy: why should such good things be
wasted ? " So she ran once more to the cellar, took another drink, and ate up the rest
of the fowl with the greatest glee.

Still her master did not come, and she cast
a lingering eye upon the other fowl, and said,
"Where the other went, this had better go too;
they belong to each other; they who have a

right to one must have a right to the other;
but if I were to take another draught first, it
would not hurt me." So she tippled down
another drop of wine, and sent the second
fowl to look after the first. While she was
making an end of this famous meal, her master came home and called out, " Now quick,
Grettel, my friend is just at hand!" " Yes,
master, I will dish up this minute," said she.
In the mean time he looked to see if the cloth
was laid, and took up the carving-knife to
sharpen it. Whilst this was going on, the
guest came and knocked softly and gently at
the house door; then Grettel ran to see who
was there, and when she saw him she put her
finger upon her lips, and said, " Hush!
hush! run away as fast as you can, for if my
master catches you, it will be worse for you;
he owes you a grudge, and asked you to
supper only that he might cut off your ears;
only listen how he is sharpening his knife."
The guest listened, and when he heard the
knife, he made as much haste as he could
down the steps and ran off. Grettel was not
idle in the mean time, but ran screaming,

"Master! master! what a fine guest you have asked to supper!" "Why, Grettel, what's the matter?" "Oh!" said she, "he has taken both the fowls that I was going to bring up, and has run away with them." "That is a rascally trick to play," said the master, sorry to lose the fine chickens; "at least he might have left me one, that I might have had something to eat; call out to him to stay." But the guest would not hear; so he ran after him with his knife in his hand, crying out, "Only one, only one, I want only one;" meaning that the guest should leave him one of the fowls, and not take both: but he thought that his host meant nothing less than that he would cut off at least one of his ears; so he ran away to save them both, as if he had hot coals under his feet.

II. *Hans in love.*

Hans's mother says to him, "Whither so fast?" "To see Grettel," says Hans. "Behave well." "Very well: Good-bye, mother!"

Hans comes to Grettel; "Good day, Grettel!" "Good day, Hans! do you bring me
any thing good?" "Nothing at all: have
you any thing for me?" Grettel gives Hans
a needle. Hans says, "Good-bye, Grettel!"
"Good-bye, Hans!" Hans takes the needle,
sticks it in a truss of hay, and takes both
off home. "Good evening, mother!" "Good
evening, Hans! where have you been?"
"To see Grettel." "What did you take
her?" "Nothing at all." "What did she
give you?" "She gave me a needle."
"Where is it, Hans?" "Stuck in the
truss." "How silly you are! you should
have stuck it in your sleeve." "Let me alone!
I'll do better next time."

"Where now, Hans?" "To see Grettel,
mother." "Behave yourself well." "Very
well: Good-bye, mother!" Hans comes to
Grettel; "Good day, Grettel!" "Good
day, Hans! what have you brought me?"
"Nothing at all: have you any thing for
me?" Grettel gives Hans a knife. "Good-
bye, Grettel!" "Good-bye, Hans!" Hans
takes the knife, sticks it in his sleeve, and goes

home. " Good evening, mother !"   " Good
evening, Hans !   where have you been ?"
" To see Grettel."   " What did you carry
her ?"   " Nothing at all."   " What has she
given you?"   " A knife."   " Where is the
knife, Hans ?"   " Stuck in my sleeve, mother."   " You silly goose ! you should have
put it in your pocket."   " Let me alone ! I 'll
do better next time."

" Where now, Hans ?"   " To see Grettel."
" Behave yourself well."   " Very well : Good-
bye, mother !"   Hans comes to Grettel ;
" Good day, Grettel !"   " Good day, Hans !
have you any thing good?"   " No : have
you any thing for me ?"   Grettel gives Hans
a kid.   " Good-bye, Grettel !"   " Good-bye,
Hans ! "   Hans takes the kid, ties it up with
a cord, stuffs it into his pocket, and chokes
it to death.   " Good evening, mother ! "
" Good evening, Hans !   where have you
been ?"   " To see Grettel, mother !"   " What
did you take her ?"   " Nothing at all."   " What
did she give you?"   " She gave me a kid."
" Where is the kid, Hans ?"   " Safe in my
pocket."   " You silly goose ! you should have

led it with a string." "Never mind, mother, I'll do better next time."

Where now, Hans?" "To Grettel's, mother." "Behave well." "Quite well, mother; Good-bye!" Hans comes to Grettel; "Good day, Grettel!" "Good day, Hans! what have you brought me?" "Nothing at all: have you any thing for me?" Grettel gives Hans a piece of bacon; Hans ties the bacon to a string and drags it behind him; the dog comes after and eats it all up as he walks home. "Good evening, mother!" "Good evening, Hans! where have you been?" "To Grettel's." "What did you take her?" "Nothing at all." "What did she give you?" "A piece of bacon." "Where is the bacon, Hans?" "Tied to the string, and dragged home, but somehow or other all gone." "What a silly trick, Hans! you should have brought it on your head." "Never mind, mother, I'll do better another time."

"Where now, Hans?" "Going to Grettel." "Take care of yourself." "Very well, mother: Good-bye." Hans comes to Grettel; —"Good day, Grettel!" "Good day, Hans!

what have you brought me?" "Nothing: have you any thing for me?" Grettel gives Hans a calf. Hans sets it upon his head, and it kicks him in the face. "Good evening, mother!" "Good evening, Hans! where have you been?" "To see Grettel." "What did you take her." "Nothing." "What did she give you?" "She gave me a calf." "Where is the calf, Hans?" "I put it on my head, and it scratched my face." "You silly goose! you should have led it home and put it in the stall." "Very well; I'll do better another time."

"Where now, Hans?" "To see Grettel." "Mind and behave well." "Good-bye, mother!" Hans comes to Grettel; "Good day, Grettel!" "Good day, Hans! what have you brought?" "Nothing at all: have you any thing for me?" "I'll go home with you." Hans ties a string round her neck, leads her along, and ties her up in the stall. "Good evening, mother!" Good evening, Hans! where have you been?" "At Grettel's." "What has she given you?" "She has come herself." "Where have you put her?"

"Fast in the stall with plenty of hay." "How silly you are! you should have taken good care of her, and brought her home." Then Hans went back to the stall; but Grettel was in a great rage, and had got loose and run away: yet, after all, she was Hans's bride.

III. *Hans married.*

Hans and Grettel lived in the village together, but Grettel did as she pleased, and was so lazy that she never would work; and when her husband gave her any yarn to spin she did it in a slovenly way; and when it was spun she did not wind it on the reel, but left it to lie all tangled about. Hans sometimes scolded, but she was always before-hand with her tongue, and said, "Why how should I wind it when I have no reel? go into the wood and make one." "If that's all," said he, "I will go into the wood and cut reel-sticks." Then Grettel was frightened lest when he had cut the sticks he should make a reel, and thus she would be forced to wind the yarn and spin again.   So she pondered a while, till at last a bright thought came into her head, and she ran slyly after her husband into the wood.   As soon as he had got into a tree and began to bend down a bough to cut it, she crept into the bush below, where he could not see her, and sung:

> " Bend not the bough ;
>   He who bends it shall die !
>   Reel not the reel;
>   He who reels it shall die ! "

Hans listened a while, laid down his axe, and thought to himself, " What can that be?" " What indeed can it be?" said he at last; "it is only a singing in your ears, Hans ! pluck up your heart, man !" So he raised up his axe again, and took hold of the bough, but once more the voice sung:

> " Bend not the bough,
>   He who bends it shall die !
>   Reel not the reel,
>   He who reels it shall die ! "

Once more he stopped his hand ; fear came over him, and he began pondering what it could mean. After a while, however, he plucked up his courage again, and took up his axe and began for the third time to cut the wood; again the third time began the song—

"Bend not the bough;
He who bends it shall die!
Reel not the reel,
He who reels it shall die!"

At this he could hold no longer, down he dropped from the tree and set off homewards as fast as he could. Away too ran Grettel by a shorter cut, so as to reach home first, and when he opened the door met him quite innocently, as if nothing had happened, and said, " Well! have you brought a good piece of wood for the reel?" " No," said he, " I see plainly that no luck comes of that reel;" and then he told her all that had happened, and left her for that time in peace.

But soon afterwards Hans began again to reproach her with the untidiness of her house. " Wife," said he; " is it not a sin and a shame that the spun yarn should lie all about

in that way?" "It may be so," said she;
"but you know very well that we have no
reel; if it must be done, lie down there and
hold up your hands and legs, and so I'll
make a reel of you, and wind off the yarn
into skeins." "Very well," said Hans (who
did not much like the job, but saw no help
for it if his wife was to be set to work); so he
did as she said, and when all was wound,
"The yarn is all in skeins," said he; "now
take care and get up early and heat the
water and boil it well, so that it may be ready for sale." Grettel disliked this part of the
work very much, but said to him, "Very
well, I'll be sure to do it very early to-morrow morning." But all the time she was
thinking to herself what plan she should take
for getting off such work for the future.

Betimes in the morning she got up, made
the fire and put on the boiler; but instead of
the yarn she laid a large ball of tow in it and
let it boil. Then she went up to her husband, who was still in bed, and said to him,
"I must go out, pray look meantime to the
yarn in the boiler over the fire; but do it

soon and take good care, for if the cock
crows and you are not looking to it, they say
it will turn to tow."   Hans soon after got up
that he might run no risk, and went (but not
perhaps as quickly as he might have done)
into the kitchen, and when he lifted up the
boiler lid and looked in, to his great terror
nothing was there but a ball of tow.   Then
off he slunk as dumb as a mouse, for he
thought to himself that he was to blame for
his laziness ; and left Grettel to get on with
her yarn and her spinning as fast as she
pleased and no faster.

One day, however, he said to her, " Wife,
I must go a little way this morning ; do you
go into the field and cut the corn."   " Yes,
to be sure, dear Hans ! " said she ; so when
he was gone she cooked herself a fine mess
and took it with her into the field.   When
she came into the field, she sat down for
a while and said to herself, " What shall I
do ? shall I sleep first or eat first ? Heigho !
I 'll first eat a bit."   Then she ate her
dinner heartily, and when she had had
enough she said again to herself, " What

shall I do ? shall I reap first or sleep first ?
Heigho ! I'll first sleep a bit." So she laid
herself down among the corn and went fast
asleep. By and by Hans came home, but no
Grettel was to be seen, and he said to himself, " What a clever wife I have ! she works
so hard that she does not even come home to
her dinner !" Evening came and still she did
not come; then Hans set off to see how much
of the corn was reaped, but there it all stood
untouched, and Grettel lay fast asleep in the
middle. So he ran home and got a string of
little bells and tied them quietly round her
waist, and went back and set himself down
on his stool and locked the house door.

At last Grettel woke when it was quite
dark, and as she rose up the bells jingled
around her every step she took. At this
she was greatly frightened, and puzzled
to tell whether she was really Grettel or not.
" Is it I, or is it not ?" said she as she stood
doubting what she ought to think. At last,
after she had pondered a while, she thought
to herself, " I will go home and ask if it is I
or not; Hans will know." So she ran to the

house door, and when she found it locked she knocked at the window and cried out, " Hans! is Grettel within?" " She is where she ought to be, to be sure," said Hans; " O dear then!" said she frightened, " this is not I." Then away she went and knocked at the neighbours' doors; but when they heard her bells rattling no one would let her in, and so at last off she ran back to the field again.

CHERRY, OR THE FROG-BRIDE.

THERE was once a king who had three sons. Not far from his kingdom lived an old woman who had an only daughter called Cherry. The king sent his sons out to see the world, that they might learn the ways of foreign lands, and get wisdom and skill in ruling the kingdom that they were one day to have for their own. But the old woman lived at peace at home with her daughter, who was called Cherry, because she liked cherries

better than any other kind of food, and
would eat scarcely any thing else. Now her
poor old mother had no garden, and no money to buy cherries every day for her daughter; and at last there was no other plan left
but to go to a neighbouring nunnery-garden
and beg the finest she could get of the nuns;
for she dared not let her daughter go out by
herself, as she was very pretty, and she feared
some mischance might befall her. Cherry's
taste was, however, very well known; and as
it happened that the abbess was as fond of
cherries as she was, it was soon found out
where all the best fruit went; and the holy
mother was not a little angry at missing some
of her stock and finding whither it had gone.

The princes while wandering on came one
day to the town where Cherry and her mother lived; and as they passed along the
street saw the fair maiden standing at the
window, combing her long and beautiful
locks of hair. Then each of the three fell
deeply in love with her, and began to say
how much he longed to have her for his wife!
Scarcely had the wish been spoken, when all

drew their swords, and a dreadful battle began; the fight lasted long, and their rage grew hotter and hotter, when at last the abbess hearing the uproar came to the gate. Finding that her neighbour was the cause, her old spite against her broke forth at once, and in her rage she wished Cherry turned into an ugly frog, and sitting in the water under the bridge at the world's end. No sooner said than done; and poor Cherry became a frog, and vanished out of their sight. The princes had now nothing to fight for; so sheathing their swords again, they shook hand as brothers, and went on towards their father's home.

The old king meanwhile found that he grew weak and ill fitted for the business of reigning: so he thought of giving up his kingdom; but to whom should it be? This was a point that his fatherly heart could not settle; for he loved all his sons alike. "My dear children," said he, "I grow old and weak, and should like to give up my kingdom; but I cannot make up my mind which of you to choose for my heir, for I love you all three;

and besides, I should wish to give my people
the cleverest and best of you for their king.
However, I will give you three trials, and
the one who wins the prize shall have the
kingdom. The first is to seek me out one
hundred ells of cloth, so fine that I can draw
it through my golden ring." The sons said
they would do their best, and set out on the
search.

The two eldest brothers took with them
many followers, and coaches and horses of
all sorts, to bring home all the beautiful
cloths which they should find; but the
youngest went alone by himself. They soon
came to where the roads branched off into
several ways; two ran through smiling meadows, with smooth paths and shady groves,
but the third looked dreary and dirty, and went
over barren wastes. The two eldest chose the
pleasant ways; and the youngest took his
leave and whistled along over the dreary road.
Whenever fine linen was to be seen, the two
elder brothers bought it, and bought so
much that their coaches and horses bent
under their burthen. The youngest, on the

other hand, journeyed on many a weary day, and found not a place where he could buy even one piece of cloth that was at all fine and good. His heart sunk beneath him, and every mile he grew more and more heavy and sorrowful. At last he came to a bridge over a stream, and there he sat himself down to rest and sigh over his bad luck, when an ugly-looking frog popped its head out of the water, and asked, with a voice that had not at all a harsh sound to his ears, what was the matter. The prince said in a pet, " Silly frog! thou canst not help me." " Who told you so?" said the frog; " tell me what ails you." After a while the prince opened the whole story, and told why his father had sent him out. " I will help you," said the frog; so it jumped back into the stream and soon came back dragging a small piece of linen not bigger than one's hand, and by no means the cleanest in the world in its look. However, there it was, and the prince was told to take it away with him. He had no great liking for such a dirty rag; but still there was something in the frog's speech that

pleased him much, and he thought to himself, " It can do no harm, it is better than
nothing;" so he picked it up, put it in his
pocket, and thanked the frog, who dived down
again, panting and quite tired, as it seemed,
with its work. The further he went the heavier
he found to his great joy the pocket grow,
and so he turned himself homewards, trusting
greatly in his good luck.

He reached home nearly about the same time
that his brothers came up, with their horses
and coaches all heavily laden.   Then the old
king was very glad to see his children again,
and pulled the ring off his finger to try who
had done the best; but in all the stock which
the two eldest had brought there was not one
piece a tenth part of which would go through
the ring.   At this they were greatly abashed;
for they had made a laugh of their brother,
who came home, as they thought, empty-
handed. But how great was their anger,
when they saw him pull from his pocket a
piece that for softness, beauty, and white-
ness, was a thousand times better than any
thing that was ever before seen !   It was so

fine that it passed with ease through the ring; indeed, two such pieces would readily have gone in together. The father embraced the lucky youth, told his servants to throw the coarse linen into the sea, and said to his children, " Now you must set about the second task which I am to set you;—bring me home a little dog, so small that it will lie in a nut-shell."

His sons were not a little frightened at such a task; but they all longed for the crown, and made up their minds to go and try their hands, and so after a few days they set out once more on their travels. At the cross-ways they parted as before, and the youngest chose his old dreary rugged road with all the bright hopes that his former good luck gave him. Scarcely had he sat himself down again at the bridge foot, when his old friend the frog jumped out, set itself beside him, and as before opened its big wide mouth, and croaked out, " What is the matter?" The prince had this time no doubt of the frog's power, and therefore told what he wanted. " It shall be done for you," said the frog;

and springing into the stream it soon brought
up a hazel-nut, laid it at his feet, and told him
to take it home to his father, and crack it
gently, and then see what would happen.
The prince went his way very well pleased,
and the frog, tired with its task, jumped back
into the water.

His brothers had reached home first, and
brought with them a great many very pretty
little dogs. The old king, willing to help
them all he could, sent for a large walnut-
shell and tried it with every one of the little
dogs; but one stuck fast with the hind-foot
out, and another with the head, and a third
with the fore-foot, and a fourth with its tail,—
in short, some one way and some another;
but none were at all likely to sit easily in this
new kind of kennel. When all had been
tried, the youngest made his father a dutiful
bow, and gave him the hazel-nut, begging
him to crack it very carefully: the moment
this was done out ran a beautiful little white
dog upon the king's hand, wagged its tail,
fondled his new master, and soon turned
about and barked at the other little beasts in

the most graceful manner, to the delight of the whole court. The joy of every one was great; the old king again embraced his lucky son, told his people to drown all the other dogs in the sea, and said to his children, " Dear sons ! your weightiest tasks are now over ; listen to my last wish ; whoever brings home the fairest lady shall be at once the heir to my crown."

The prize was so tempting and the chance so fair for all, that none made any doubts about setting to work, each in his own way, to try and be the winner. The youngest was not in such good spirits as he was the last time; he thought to himself, " The old frog has been able to do a great deal for me; but all its power must be nothing to me now, for where should it find me a fair maiden, still less a fairer maiden than was ever seen at my father's court ? The swamps where it lives have no living things in them, but toads, snakes, and such vermin." Meantime he went on, and sighed as he sat down again with a heavy heart by the bridge. " Ah frog !" said he, " this time thou canst do me no good." " Never mind," croaked the frog; "only tell me what is the matter now." Then the prince told his old friend what trouble had now come upon him. " Go thy ways home," said the frog; " the fair maiden will follow hard after; but take care and do not laugh at whatever may happen!" This said, it sprang as before into the water and was soon out of sight. The prince still sighed on, for he trusted very little this time to the frog's word; but he had not set many steps towards home before he heard a noise behind him, and looking round saw six large water rats dragging along a large pumpkin like a coach, full trot. On the box sat an old fat toad as coachman, and behind stood two little frogs as footmen, and two fine mice with stately whiskers ran before as outriders; within sat his old friend the frog, rather misshapen and unseemly to be sure, but still with somewhat of a graceful air as it bowed to him in passing. Much too deeply wrapt in thought as to his chance of finding the fair lady whom he was seeking, to take any heed of the strange scene before him, the prince

G Cruikshank

scarcely looked at it, and had still less mind to laugh. The coach passed on a little way, and soon turned a corner that hid it from his sight; but how astonished was he, on turning the corner himself, to find a handsome coach and six black horses standing there, with a coachman in gay livery, and within, the most beautiful lady he had ever seen, whom he soon knew to be the fair Cherry, for whom his heart had so long ago panted! As he came up, the servants opened the coach door, and he was allowed to seat himself by the beautiful lady.

They soon came to his father's city, where his brothers also came, with trains of fair ladies; but as soon as Cherry was seen, all the court gave her with one voice the crown of beauty. The delighted father embraced his son, and named him the heir to his crown, and ordered all the other ladies to be thrown like the little dogs into the sea and drowned. Then the prince married Cherry, and lived long and happily with her, and indeed lives with her still—if he be not dead.

MOTHER HOLLE.

A widow had two daughters; one of them was very pretty and thrifty, but the other was ugly and idle.

Odd as you may think it, she loved the ugly and idle one much the best, and the other was made to do all the work, and was in short quite the drudge of the whole house. Every day she had to sit on a bench by a well on the side of the high-road before the house, and spin so much that her fingers were quite sore, and at length the blood would come. Now it happened that once when her fingers had bled and the spindle was all bloody, she dipt it into the well, and meant to wash it, but unluckily it fell from her hand and dropt in. Then she ran crying to her mother, and told her what had happened; but she scolded her sharply, and said, "If you have been so silly as to let the spindle fall in, you must get it out again as well as you can." So the poor little girl went back to the well, and knew not how to begin, but

in her sorrow threw herself into the water,
and sank down to the bottom senseless.   In
a short time she seemed to awake as from a
trance, and came to herself again ; and when
she opened her eyes and looked around, she
saw she was in a beautiful meadow, where the
sun shone brightly, the birds sang sweetly
on the boughs, and thousands of flowers
sprang beneath her feet.

Then she rose up, and walked along
this delightful meadow, and came to a pretty
cottage by the side of a wood ; and when she
went in she saw an oven full of new bread
baking, and the bread said, " Pull me out !
pull me out ! or I shall be burnt, for I am
quite done enough." So she stepped up
quickly and took it all out.   Then she went
on further, and came to a tree that was full of
fine rosy cheeked apples, and it said to her,
" Shake me ! shake me ! we are all quite
ripe ! "   So she shook the tree, and the apples fell down like a shower, until there were
no more upon the tree.   Then she went on
again, and at length came to a small cottage
where an old woman was sitting at the door :

the little girl would have run away, but the old woman called out after her, " Don't be frightened, my dear child ! stay with me, I should like to have you for my little maid, and if you do all the work in the house neatly you shall fare well; but take care to make my bed nicely, and shake it every morning out at the door, so that the feathers may fly, for then the good people below say it snows.—I am Mother Holle."

As the old woman spoke so kindly to her, the girl was willing to do as she said; so she went into her employ, and took care to do every thing to please her, and always shook the bed well, so that she led a very quiet life with her, and every day had good meat both boiled and roast to eat for her dinner.

But when she had been some time with the old lady, she became sorrowful, and although she was much better off here than at home, still she had a longing towards it, and at length said to her mistress, " I used to grieve at my troubles at home, but if they were all to come again, and I were sure of faring ever so well here, I could not stay any longer." "You are right," said her mistress; "you shall do as you like; and as you have worked for me so faithfully, I will myself show you the way back again." Then she took her by the hand and led her behind her cottage, and opened a door, and as the girl stood underneath there fell a heavy shower of gold, so that she held out her apron and caught a great deal of it. And the fairy put a shining golden dress over her, and said, "All this you shall have because you have behaved so well;" and she gave her back the spindle too which had fallen into the well, and led her out by another door. When it shut behind her, she found herself not far from her mother's house; and as she went into the court-yard the cock sat upon the well-head and clapt his wings and cried out,

"Cock a-doodle-doo !
Our golden lady 's come home again."

Then she went into the house, and as she was so rich she was welcomed home. When her mother heard how she got these riches, she wanted to have the same luck for her

ugly and idle daughter, so she too was told
to sit by the well and spin. That her spindle might be bloody, she pricked her fingers
with it, and when that would not do she
thrust her hand into a thorn-bush. Then
she threw it into the well and sprung in herself after it. Like her sister, she came to a
beautiful meadow, and followed the same
path. When she came to the oven in the
cottage, the bread called out as before, "Take
me out! take me out! or I shall burn, I
am quite done enough." But the lazy girl
said, " A pretty story, indeed! just as if I
should dirty myself for you!" and went on
her way. She soon came to the apple-tree
that cried, "Shake me! shake me! for my
apples are quite ripe!" but she answered,
" I will take care how I do that, for one of
you might fall upon my head;" so she went
on. At length she came to Mother Holle's
house, and readily agreed to be her maid.
The first day she behaved herself very well,
and did what her mistress told her; for she
thought of the gold she would give her; but
the second day she began to be lazy, and the

third still more so, for she would not get up in the morning early enough, and when she did she made the bed very badly, and did not shake it so that the feathers would fly out. Mother Holle was soon tired of her, and turned her off; but the lazy girl was quite pleased at that, and thought to herself, " Now the golden rain will come." Then the fairy took her to the same door ; but when she stood under it, instead of gold a great kettle full of dirty pitch came showering upon her. " That is your wages," said Mother Holle as she shut the door upon her. So she went home quite black with the pitch, and as she came near her mother's house the cock sat upon the well, and clapt his wings, and cried out—

" Cock a-doodle-doo !
Our dirty slut 's come home again ! "

THE WATER OF LIFE.

Long before you and I were born there reigned, in a country a great way off, a king who had three sons. This king once fell very ill, so ill that nobody thought he could live. His sons were very much grieved at their father's sickness; and as they walked weeping in the garden of the palace, an old man met them and asked what they ailed. They told him their father was so ill that they were afraid nothing could save him. " I know what would," said the old man; " it is the Water of Life. If he could have a draught of it he would be well again, but it is very hard to get." Then the eldest son said, " I will soon find it," and went to the sick king, and begged that he might go in search of the Water of Life, as it was the only thing that could save him. " No," said the king; " I had rather die than place you in such great danger as you must meet with in your journey." But he begged so hard that the king let him go; and the prince thought to himself, " If I bring my father this water I shall be his dearest son, and he will make me heir to his kingdom."

Then he set out, and when he had gone on his way some time he came to a deep valley overhung with rocks and woods; and as he looked around there stood above him on one of the rocks a little dwarf, who called out to him and said, " Prince, whither hastest thou so fast?" " What is that to you, little ugly one?" said the prince sneeringly, and rode on his way. But the little dwarf fell into a great rage at his behaviour, and laid a spell of ill luck upon him, so that, as he rode on, the mountain pass seemed to become narrower and narrower, and at last the way was so straitened that he could not go a step forward, and when he thought to have turned his horse round and gone back the way he came, the passage he found had closed behind also, and shut him quite up; he next tried to get off his horse and make his way on foot, but this he was unable to do, and so there he was forced to abide spell-bound.

Meantime the king his father was lingering

on in daily hope of his return, till at last the second son said, " Father, I will go in search of this Water;" for he thought to himself, " My brother is surely dead, and the kingdom will fall to me if I have good luck in my journey." The king was at first very unwilling to let him go, but at last yielded to his wish. So he set out and followed the same road which his brother had taken, and met the same dwarf, who stopped him at the same spot, and said as before, " Prince, whither hastest thou so fast?" " Mind your own affairs, busy body!" answered the prince scornfully, and rode off. But the dwarf put the same enchantment upon him, and when he came like the other to the narrow pass in the mountains he could neither move forward nor backward. Thus it is with proud silly people, who think themselves too wise to take advice.

When the second prince had thus staid away a long while, the youngest said he would go and search for the Water of Life, and trusted he should soon be able to make his father well again. The dwarf met him too at the same spot, and said, " Prince, whither hastest thou so fast?" and the prince said, " I go in search of the Water of Life, because my father is ill and like to die:—can you help me?" " Do you know where it is to be found?" asked the dwarf. " No," said the prince. " Then as you have spoken to me kindly and sought for advice, I will tell you how and where to go. The Water you seek springs from a well in an enchanted castle, and that you may be able to go in safety I will give you an iron wand and two little loaves of bread; strike the iron door of the castle three times with the wand, and it will open : two hungry lions will be lying down inside gaping for their prey; but if you throw them the bread they will let you pass; then hasten on to the well and take some of the Water of Life before the clock strikes twelve, for if you tarry longer the door will shut upon you for ever."

Then the prince thanked the dwarf for his friendly aid, and took the wand and the bread and went travelling on and on over sea and land, till he came to his journey's end, and found every thing to be as the dwarf had told him. The door flew open at the third stroke of the wand, and when the lions were quieted he went on through the castle, and came at length to a beautiful hall; around it he saw several knights sitting in a trance; then he pulled off their rings and put them on his own fingers. In another room he saw on a table a sword and a loaf of bread, which he also took. Further on he came to a room where a beautiful young lady sat upon a couch, who welcomed him joyfully, and said, if he would set her free from the spell that bound her, the kingdom should be his if he would come back in a year and marry her; then she told him that the well that held the Water of Life was in the palace gardens, and bade him make haste and draw what he wanted before the clock struck twelve. Then he went on, and as he walked through beautiful gardens he came to a delightful shady spot in which stood a couch; and he thought to himself, as he felt tired, that he would rest himself for a while and gaze on the lovely scenes around him. So he laid himself down,

and sleep fell upon him unawares and he did
not wake up till the clock was striking a quarter
to twelve; then he sprung from the couch
dreadfully frightened, ran to the well, filled a
cup that was standing by him full of Water,
and hastened to get away in time. Just as
he was going out of the iron door it struck
twelve, and the door fell so quickly upon him
that it tore away a piece of his heel.

When he found himself safe he was overjoyed to think that he had got the Water of
Life; and as he was going on his way homewards, he passed by the little dwarf, who when
he saw the sword and the loaf said, " You
have made a noble prize; with the sword you
can at a blow slay whole armies, and the
bread will never fail." Then the prince
thought to himself, " I cannot go home to
my father without my brothers;" so he said,
" Dear dwarf, cannot you tell me where my
two brothers are, who set out in search of the
Water of Life before me and never came
back?" "I have shut them up by a charm
between two mountains," said the dwarf,
" because they were proud and ill behaved,

and scorned to ask advice." The prince begged so hard for his brothers that the dwarf at last set them free, though unwillingly, saying, " Beware of them, for they have bad hearts." Their brother, however, was greatly rejoiced to see them, and told them all that had happened to him, how he had found the Water of Life, and had taken a cup full of it, and how he had set a beautiful princess free from a spell that bound her ; and how she had engaged to wait a whole year, and then to marry him and give him the kingdom. Then they all three rode on together, and on their way home came to a country that was laid waste by war and a dreadful famine, so that it was feared all must die for want. But the prince gave the king of the land the bread, and all his kingdom ate of it. And he slew the enemy's army with the wonderful sword, and left the kingdom in peace and plenty. In the same manner he befriended two other countries that they passed through on their way.

When they came to the sea, they got into a ship, and during their voyage the two eldest said to themselves, " Our brother has got the Water which we could not find, therefore our father will forsake us, and give him the kingdom which is our right;" so they were full of envy and revenge, and agreed together how they could ruin him. They waited till he was fast asleep, and then poured the Water of Life out of the cup and took it for themselves, giving him bitter sea-water instead. And when they came to their journey's end, the youngest son brought his cup to the sick king, that he might drink and be healed. Scarcely, however, had he tasted the bitter sea-water when he became worse even than he was before, and then both the elder sons came in and blamed the youngest for what he had done, and said that he wanted to poison their father, but that they had found the Water of Life and had brought it with them. He no sooner began to drink of what they brought him, than he felt his sickness leave him, and was as strong and well as in his young days; then they went to their brother and laughed at him, and said, " Well, brother, you found the Water of

Life, did you? you have had the trouble and we shall have the reward; pray, with all your cleverness why did not you manage to keep your eyes open? Next year one of us will take away your beautiful princess, if you do not take care; you had better say nothing about this to our father, for he does not believe a word you say, and if you tell tales, you shall lose your life into the bargain, but be quiet and we will let you off."

The old king was still very angry with his youngest son, and thought that he really meant to have taken away his life; so he called his court together and asked what should be done, and it was settled that he should be put to death. The prince knew nothing of what was going on, till one day when the king's chief huntsman went a-hunting with him, and they were alone in the wood together, the huntsman looked so sorrowful that the prince said, "My friend, what is the matter with you?" "I cannot and dare not tell you," said he. But the prince begged hard and said, "Only say what it is, and do not think I shall be angry, for I will forgive you." "Alas!" said the huntsman, "the king has ordered me to shoot you." The prince started at this, and said, "Let me live, and I will change dresses with you; you shall take my royal coat to show to my father, and do you give me your shabby one." "With all my heart," said the huntsman; "I am sure I shall be glad to save you, for I could not have shot you." Then he took the prince's coat, and gave him the shabby one, and went away through the wood.

Some time after, three grand embassies came to the old king's court, with rich gifts of gold and precious stones for his youngest son, which were sent from the three kings to whom he had lent his sword and loaf of bread, to rid them of their enemy, and feed their people. This touched the old king's heart, and he thought his son might still be guiltless, and said to his court, "Oh! that my son were still alive! how it grieves me that I had him killed!" "He still lives," said the huntsman; "and I rejoice that I had pity on him, and saved him, for when the time came, I could not shoot him, but let him go in peace and brought home his royal coat." At this the king was overwhelmed with joy, and made it known throughout all his kingdom, that if his son would come back to his court, he would forgive him.

Meanwhile the princess was eagerly waiting the return of her deliverer, and had a road made leading up to her palace all of shining gold; and told her courtiers that whoever came on horseback and rode straight up to the gate upon it, was her true lover, and that they must let him in; but whoever rode on one side of it, they must be sure was not the right one, and must send him away at once.

The time soon came, when the eldest thought he would make haste to go to the princess, and say that he was the one who had set her free, and that he should have her for his wife, and the kingdom with her. As he came before the palace and saw the golden road, he stopt to look at it, and thought to himself, " It is a pity to ride

upon this beautiful road;" so he turned
aside and rode on the right of it. But when
he came to the gate, the guards said to him,
he was not what he said he was, and must go
about his business. The second prince set
out soon afterwards on the same errand; and
when he came to the golden road, and his
horse had set one foot upon it, he stopt to
look at it, and thought it very beautiful, and
said to himself, " What a pity it is that any
thing should tread here !" then he too turned aside and rode on the left of it. But
when he came to the gate the guards said he
was not the true prince, and that he too
must go away.

Now when the full year was come, the
third brother left the wood, where he had
laid for fear of his father's anger, and set
out in search of his betrothed bride. So he
journeyed on, thinking of her all the way, and
rode so quickly that he did not even see the
golden road, but went with his horse straight
over it; and as he came to the gate, it flew
open, and the princess welcomed him with
joy, and said he was her deliverer and should

now be her husband and lord of the kingdom, and the marriage was soon kept with
great feasting. When it was over, the princess told him she had heard of his father
having forgiven him, and of his wish to have
him home again: so he went to visit him,
and told him every thing, how his brothers
had cheated and robbed him, and yet that
he had borne all these wrongs for the love of
his father. Then the old king was very
angry, and wanted to punish his wicked sons;
but they made their escape, and got into a
ship and sailed away ove.· the wide sea, and
were r.ever heard of any more.

PETER THE GOATHERD.

IN the wilds of the Hartz Forest there is a
high mountain, where the fairies and goblins
dance by night, and where they say the great
Emperor Frederic Barbarossa still holds his
court among the caverns. Now and then he
shows himself and punishes those whom he
dislikes, or gives some rich gift to the lucky

wight whom he takes it into his head to be-
friend. He sits on a throne of marble with
his red beard sweeping on the ground, and
once or twice in a long course of years rouses
himself for a while from the trance in which
he is buried, but soon falls again into his
former forgetfulness. Strange chances have
befallen many who have strayed within the
range of his court:—you shall hear one of
them.

A great many years ago there lived in the
village at the foot of the mountain, one Peter,
a goatherd. Every morning he drove his
flock to feed upon the green spots that are
here and there found on the mountain's side,
and in the evening he sometimes thought it
too far to drive his charge home, so he used
in such cases to shut it up in a spot amongst
the woods, where an old ruined wall was left
standing, high enough to form a fold, in
which he could count his goats and rest in
peace for the night. One evening he found
that the prettiest goat of his flock had vanished
soon after they were driven into this fold,
but was there again in the morning. Again

and again he watched, and the same strange
thing happened.   He thought he would look
still more narrowly, and soon found a cleft in
the old wall, through which it seemed that his
favourite made her way.   Peter followed,
scrambling as well as he could down the
side of the rock, and wondered not a little,
on overtaking his goat, to find it employing
itself very much at its ease in a cavern, eating corn, which kept dropping from some
place above.   He went into the cavern and
looked about him to see where all this corn,
that rattled about his ears like a hail storm,
could come from: but all was dark, and he
could find no clue to this strange business.
At last, as he stood listening, he thought he
heard the neighing and stamping of horses.
He listened again; it was plainly so; and after
a while he was sure that horses were feeding
above him, and that the corn fell from their
mangers. What could these horses be, which
were thus kept in a mountain where none
but the goat's foot ever trod? Peter pondered a while; but his wonder only grew
greater and greater, when on a sudden a lit-

tle page came forth and beckoned him to
follow; he did so, and came at last to a court-
yard surrounded by an old wall. The spot
seemed the bosom of the valley; above rose
on every hand high masses of rock; wide
branching trees threw their arms over head,
so that nothing but a glimmering twilight
made its way through; and here, on the cool
smooth shaven turf, were twelve old knights,
who looked very grave and sober, but were
amusing themselves with a game of nine-pins.

Not a word fell from their lips; but they
ordered Peter by dumb signs to busy himself in setting up the pins, as they knocked
them down. At first his knees trembled, as
he dared to snatch a stolen sidelong glance
at the long beards and old-fashioned dresses
of the worthy knights. Little by little, however, he grew bolder; and at last he plucked
up his heart so far as to take his turn in the
draught at the can, which stood beside him
and sent up the smell of the richest old wine.
This gave him new strength for his work;
and as often as he flagged at all, he turned
to the same kind friend for help in his need.

Sleep at last overpowered him; and when he awoke he found himself stretched out upon the old spot where he had folded his flock. The same green turf was spread beneath, and the same tottering walls surrounded him: he rubbed his eyes, but neither dog nor goat was to be seen, and when he had looked about him again the grass seemed to be longer under his feet, and trees hung over his head which he had either never seen before or had forgotten. Shaking his head, and hardly knowing whether he were in his right mind, he wound his way among the mountain steeps, through paths where his flocks were wont to wander; but still not a goat was to be seen. Below him in the plain lay the village where his home was, and at length he took the downward path, and set out with a heavy heart in search of his flock. The people who met him as he drew near to the village were all unknown to him; they were not even drest as his neighbours were, and they seemed as if they hardly spoke the same tongue; and when he eagerly asked after his goats, they only stared at him and stroked their chins. At last he did the same too, and what was his wonder to find that his beard was grown at least a foot long! The world, thought he now to himself, is turned over, or at any rate bewitched; and yet he knew the mountain (as he turned round to gaze upon its woody heights); and he knew the houses and cottages also, with their little gardens, all of which were in the same places as he had always known them; he heard some children, too, call the village by its old name, as a traveller that passed by was asking his way.

Again he shook his head and went straight through the village to his own cottage. Alas! it looked sadly out of repair; and in the court-yard lay an unknown child, in a ragged dress, by the side of a rough, toothless dog, whom he thought he ought to know, but who snarled and barked in his face when he called him to him. He went in at an opening in the wall where a door had once stood, but found all so dreary and empty that he staggered out again like a drunken man, and called his wife and children loudly by their names; but no one heard, at least no one answered him.

A crowd of women and children soon flocked around the long gray bearded man, and all broke upon him at once with the questions, " Who are you ? " " Whom do you want ? " It seemed to him so odd to ask other people at his own door after his wife and children, that in order to get rid of the crowd he named the first man that came into his head; —" Hans, the blacksmith ! " said he. Most held their tongues and stared, but at last an old woman said, " He went these seven years ago to a place that you will not reach to-day." " Frank the tailor, then ! " " Heaven rest his soul ! " said an old beldame upon crutches; " he has laid these ten years in a house that he 'll never leave."

Peter looked at the old woman, and shuddered as he saw her to be one of his old friends, only with a strangely altered face, All wish to ask further questions was gone; but at last a young woman made her way through the gaping throng with a baby in her arms, and a little girl about three years old clinging to her other hand; all three looked the very image of his wife. "What is thy name?" asked he wildly. "Mary." "And your father's?" "Heaven bless him! Peter! It is now twenty years since we sought him day and night on the mountain; his flock came back, but he never was heard of any more. I was then seven years old." The goatherd could hold no longer. "I am Peter," cried he; "I am Peter, and no other;" as he took the child from his daughter's arms and kissed it. All stood gaping, and not knowing what to say or think, till at length one voice was heard, "Why it is Peter!" and then several others cried, "Yes, it is, it is Peter! Welcome neighbour, welcome home, after twenty long years!"

THE FOUR CLEVER BROTHERS.

"Dear children," said a poor man to his four sons, "I have nothing to give you; you must go out into the world, and try your luck.

Begin by learning some trade, and see how you can get on." So the four brothers took their walking-sticks in their hands, and their little bundles on their shoulders, and, after bidding their father good-bye, went all out at the gate together. When they had got on some way they came to four cross-ways, each leading to a different country. Then the eldest said, "Here we must part; but this day four years we will come back to this spot; and in the mean time each must try what he can do for himself." So each brother went his way; and as the oldest was hastening on, a man met him, and asked him where he was going and what he wanted. "I am going to try my luck in the world, and should like to begin by learning some trade," answered he. "Then," said the man, "go with me, and I will teach you how to become the cunningest thief that ever was." "No," said the other, "that is not an honest calling, and what can one look to earn by it in the end but the gallows?" "Oh!" said the man, "you need not fear the gallows; for I will only teach you to steal what will be fair game; I meddle with nothing but what no one else can get or care any thing about, and where no one can find you out." So the young man agreed to follow his trade, and he soon showed himself so clever that nothing could escape him that he had once set his mind upon.

The second brother also met a man, who, when he found out what he was setting out upon, asked him what trade he meant to learn. " I do not know yet," said he. "Then come with me, and be a star-gazer. It is a noble trade, for nothing can be hidden from you when you understand the stars." The plan pleased him much, and he soon became such a skilful star-gazer, that when he had served out his time, and wanted to leave his master, he gave him a glass, and said, " With this you can see all that is passing in the sky and on earth, and nothing can be hidden from you."

The third brother met a huntsman, who took him with him, and taught him so well all that belonged to hunting, that he became very clever in that trade; and when he left his master he gave him a bow, and said, " Whatever you shoot at with this bow you will be sure to hit."

The youngest brother likewise met a man who asked him what he wished to do. " Would not you like," said he, " to be a tailor?" " Oh no!" said the young man; " sitting cross-legged from morning to night, working backwards and forwards with a needle and goose, will never suit me." " Oh!" answered the man, " that is not my sort of tailoring; come with me, and you will learn quite another kind of trade from that." Not knowing what better to do, he came into the plan, and learnt the trade from the beginning; and when he left his master, he gave him a needle, and said, " You can sew any thing with this, be it as soft as an egg, or as hard as steel, and the joint will be so fine that no seam will be seen."

After the space of four years, at the time agreed upon, the four brothers met at the four cross-roads, and having welcomed each other, set off towards their father's home, where they told him all that had happened to them, and how each had learned some trade. Then one day, as they were sitting before the house under a very high tree, the father said, " I should like to try what each of you can do in his trade." So he looked up, and said to the second son, " At the top of this tree there is a chaffinch's nest ; tell me how many eggs there are in it." The star-gazer took his glass, looked up, and said, " Five." " Now," said the father to the eldest son, " take away the eggs without the bird that is sitting upon them and hatching them, knowing any thing of what you are doing." So the cunning thief climbed up the tree, and brought away to his father the five eggs from under the bird, who never saw or felt what he was doing, but kept sitting on at her ease. Then the father took the eggs, and put one on each corner of the table and the fifth in the middle, and said to the huntsman, " Cut all the eggs in two pieces at one shot." The huntsman took up his bow, and at one shot struck all the five eggs as his father wished. " Now comes your turn," said he to the young tailor ; " sew the eggs and the young birds

in them together again, so neatly that the
shot shall have done them no harm." Then
the tailor took his needle and sewed the eggs
as he was told; and when he had done, the
thief was sent to take them back to the nest,
and put them under the bird, without its
knowing it. Then she went on setting, and
hatched them; and in a few days they crawled
out, and had only a little red streak across
their necks where the tailor had sewed them
together.

"Well done, sons!" said the old man,
"you have made good use of your time, and
learnt something worth the knowing; but I
am sure I do not know which ought to have
the prize. Oh! that a time might soon come
for you to turn your skill to some account!"

Not long after this there was a great bustle
in the country; for the king's daughter had
been carried off by a mighty dragon, and the
king mourned over his loss day and night,
and made it known that whoever brought her
back to him should have her for a wife.
Then the four brothers said to each other,
"Here is a chance for us; let us try what we

can do." And they agreed to see whether they could not set the princess free. " I will soon find out where she is, however," said the star-gazer as he looked through his glass, and soon cried out, " I see her afar off, sitting upon a rock in the sea, and I can spy the dragon close by, guarding her." Then he went to the king, and asked for a ship for himself and his brothers, and went with them upon the sea till they came to the right place. There they found the princess sitting, as the star-gazer had said, on the rock, and the dragon was lying asleep with his head upon her lap. " I dare not shoot at him," said the huntsman, " for I should kill the beautiful young lady also." " Then I will try my skill," said the thief; and went and stole her away from under the dragon so quickly and gently that the beast did not know it, but went on snoring.

Then away they hastened with her full of joy in their boat towards the ship; but soon came the dragon roaring behind them through the air, for he awoke and missed the princess:

but when he got over the boat, and wanted to pounce upon them and carry off the princess, the huntsman took up his bow and shot him straight at the heart, so that he fell down dead. They were still not safe; for he was such a great beast, that in his fall he overset the boat, and they had to swim in the open sea upon a few planks. So the tailor took his needle, and with a few large stitches put some of the planks together, and sat down upon them, and sailed about and gathered up all the pieces of the boat, and tacked them together so quickly that the boat was soon ready, and they then reached the ship and got home safe.

When they had brought home the princess to her father, there was great rejoicing; and he said to the four brothers, "One of you shall marry her, but you must settle amongst yourselves which it is to be." Then there arose a quarrel between them; and the star-gazer said, "If I had not found the princess out, all your skill would have been of no use; therefore she ought to be mine." "Your

seeing her would have been of no use," said
the thief, "if I had not taken her away from
the dragon; therefore she ought to be mine."
"No, she is mine," said the huntsman; "for
if I had not killed the dragon, he would after
all have torn you and the princess into pieces."
"And if I had not sewed the boat together
again," said the tailor, "you would all have
been drowned; therefore she is mine." Then
the king put in a word, and said, "Each of
you is right; and as all cannot have the
young lady, the best way is for neither of you
to have her; and to make up for the loss,
I will give each, as a reward for his skill,
half a kingdom." So the brothers agreed
that would be much better than quarrelling;
and the king then gave each half a kingdom,
as he had said; and they lived very happily
the rest of their days, and took good care of
their father.

THE ELFIN-GROVE.

" I hope," said a woodman one day to his wife, " that the children will not run into that fir-grove by the side of the river; who they are that have come to live there I cannot tell, but I am sure it looks more dark and gloomy than ever, and some queer-looking beings are to be seen lurking about it every night, as I am told." The woodman could not say that they brought any ill luck as yet, whatever they were; for all the village had thriven more than ever since they came; the fields looked gayer and greener, and even the sky was a deeper blue. Not knowing what to say of them, the farmer very wisely let his new friends alone, and in truth troubled his head very little about them.

That very evening little Mary and her playfellow Martin were playing at hide and seek in the valley. " Where can he be hid?" said she; " he must have gone into the fir grove," and down she ran to look. Just then she spied a little dog that jumped round her

and wagged his tail, and led her on towards
the wood. Then he ran into it, and she
soon jumped up the bank to look after him,
but was overjoyed to see, instead of a gloomy
grove of firs, a delightful garden, where
flowers and shrubs of every kind grew upon
turf of the softest green; gay butterflies flew
about her, the birds sang sweetly, and, what
was strangest, the prettiest little children
sported about on all sides, some twining the
flowers, and others dancing in rings upon the
shady spots beneath the trees. In the midst,
instead of the hovels of which Mary had
heard, there was a palace that dazzled her eyes
with its brightness. For a while she gazed
on the fairy scene around her, till at last
one of the little dancers ran up to her, and
said, " And you are come at last to see us?
we have often seen you play about, and wished
to have you with us." Then she plucked
some of the fruit that grew near; and Mary
at the first taste forgot her home, and wished
only to see and know more of her fairy
friends.

Then they led her about with them and

showed her all their sports.   One while they
danced by moonlight on the primrose banks;
at another time they skipped from bough to
bough among the trees that hung over the
cooling streams; for they moved as lightly
and easily through the air as on the ground:
and Mary went with them every where, for
they bore her in their arms wherever they
wished to go.   Sometimes they would throw
seeds on the turf, and directly little trees
sprung up; and then they would set their feet
upon the branches, while the trees grew under
them, till they danced upon the boughs in the
air, wherever the breezes carried them; and
again the trees would sink down into the
earth and land them safely at their bidding.
At other times they would go and visit the
palace of their queen; and there the richest
food was spread before them, and the softest
music was heard; and there all around grew
flowers which were always changing their
hues, from scarlet to purple and yellow and
emerald.   Sometimes they went to look at the
heaps of treasure which were piled up in the
royal stores; for little dwarfs were always em-

ployed in searching the earth for gold. Small as this fairy land looked from without, it seemed within to have no end; a mist hung around it to shield it from the eyes of men; and some of the little elves sat perched upon the outermost trees, to keep watch lest the step of man should break in and spoil the charm.

" And who are you?" said Mary one day. " We are what are called elves in your world," said one whose name was Gossamer, and who had become her dearest friend : " we are told you talk a great deal about us; some of our tribes like to work you mischief, but we who live here seek only to be happy : we meddle little with mankind; but when we do come among them, it is to do them good." "And where is your queen?" said little Mary. " Hush ! hush ! you cannot see or know her : you must leave us before she comes back, which will be now very soon, for mortal step cannot come where she is. But you will know that she is here when you see the meadows gayer, the rivers more sparkling, and the sun brighter."

Soon afterwards Gossamer told Mary the

time was come to bid her farewell, and gave
her a ring in token of their friendship, and
led her to the edge of the grove. " Think
of me," said she ; " but beware how you tell
what you have seen, or try to visit any of us
again, for if you do, we shall quit this grove
and come back no more." Turning back, Mary
saw nothing but the gloomy fir-grove she had
known before. " How frightened my father and
mother will be !" thought she as she looked
at the sun, which had risen some time. "They
will wonder where I have been all night, and
yet I must not tell them what I have seen."
She hastened homewards, wondering however, as she went, to see that the leaves, which
were yesterday so fresh and green, were now
falling dry and yellow around her. The cottage too seemed changed, and, when she
went in, there sat her father looking some
years older than when she saw him last ; and
her mother, whom she hardly knew, was by
his side. Close by was a young man ; " Father," said Mary, " who is this ?" " Who
are you that call me father ?" said he ; " are
you—no you cannot be—our long-lost Mary ?"

But they soon saw that it was their Mary; and the young man, who was her old friend and playfellow Martin, said, "No wonder you had forgotten me in seven years; do not you remember how we parted seven years ago while playing in the field? We thought you were quite lost; but we are glad to see that some one has taken care of you and brought you home at last." Mary said nothing, for she could not tell all; but she wondered at the strange tale, and felt gloomy at the change from fairy land to her father's cottage.

Little by little she came to herself, thought of her story as a mere dream, and soon became Martin's bride. Every thing seemed to thrive around them; and Mary called her first little girl Elfie, in memory of her friends. The little thing was loved by every one. It was pretty and very good-tempered; Mary thought that it was very like a little elf; and all, without knowing why, called it the fairy child.

One day, while Mary was dressing her little Elfie, she found a piece of gold hanging

round her neck by a silken thr l, and
knew it to be of the same sort as she had
seen in the hands of the fairy dwarfs. Elfie
seemed sorry at its being seen, and said that she
had found it in the garden. But Mary watched
her, and soon found that she went every afternoon to sit by herself in a shady place behind
the house : so one day she hid herself to see
what the child did there ; and to her great wonder Gossamer was sitting by her side. " Dear
Elfie," she was saying, " your mother and I
used to sit thus when she was young and
lived among us.   Oh ! if you could but come
and do so too ! but since our queen came to
us it cannot be; yet I will come and see you
and talk to you, whilst you are a child; when
you grow up we must part for ever."   Then
she plucked one of the roses that grew
around them and breathed gently upon it,
and said " Take this for my sake. It will
keep its freshness a whole year."

Then Mary loved her little Elfie more than
ever ; and when she found that she spent
some hours of almost every day with the elf,
she used to hide herself and watch them with-

out being seen, till one day when Gossamer was bearing her little friend through the air from tree to tree, her mother was so frightened lest her child should fall that she could not help screaming out, and Gossamer set her gently on the ground and seemed angry, and flew away. But still she used sometimes to come and play with her little friend, and would soon have done so perhaps the same as before, had not Mary one day told her husband the whole story, for she could not bear to hear him always wondering and laughing at their little child's odd ways, and saying he was sure there was something in the fir-grove that brought them no good. So to show him that all she said was true, she took him to see Elfie and the fairy; but no sooner did Gossamer know that he was there, (which she did in an instant,) than she changed herself into a raven and flew off into the fir-grove.

Mary burst into tears, and so did Elfie, for she knew she should see her dear friend no more: but Martin was restless and bent upon following up his search after the fairies; so

when night came he stole away towards the
grove. When he came to it nothing was to
be seen but the gloomy firs and the old
hovels; and the thunder rolled, and the
wind groaned and whistled through the trees.
It seemed that all about him was angry;
so he turned homewards frightened at what
he had done.

In the morning all the neighbours flocked
around, asking one another what the noise
and bustle of the last night could mean; and
when they looked about them, their trees
looked blighted, and the meadows parched,
the streams were dried up, and every thing
seemed troubled and sorrowful; but they all
thought that some how or other the fir-grove
had not near so forbidding a look as it used
to have. Strange stories were told, how one
had heard flutterings in the air, another had
seen the fir-grove as it were alive with
little beings that flew away from it. Each
neighbour told his tale, and all wondered
what could have happened; but Mary and
her husband knew what was the matter, and
bewailed their folly; for they foresaw that

their kind neighbours, to whom they owed all their luck, were gone for ever. Among the bystanders none told a wilder story than the old ferryman who plied across the river at the foot of the grove; he told how at midnight his boat was carried away, and how hundreds of little beings seemed to load it with treasures; how a strange piece of gold was left for him in the boat, as his fare; how the air seemed full of fairy forms fluttering around; and how at last a great train passed over that seemed to be guarding their leader to the meadows on the other side; and how he heard soft music floating around as they flew; and how sweet voices sang as they hovered over his head,

> Fairy Queen!
> Fairy Queen!
> Mortal steps are on the green;
> Come away!
> Haste away!
> Fairies, guard your Queen!
> Hither, hither, fairy Queen!
> Lest thy silvery wing be seen;

O'er the sky
Fly, fly, fly !
Fairies, guard your lady Queen !
O'er the sky
Fly, fly, fly !
Fairies, guard your Queen !

Fairy Queen !
Fairy Queen !
Thou hast pass'd the treach'rous scene ;
Now we may
Down and play
O'er the daisied green.
Lightly, lightly, fairy Queen !
Trip it gently o'er the green :
Fairies gay,
Trip away
Round about your lady Queen !
Fairies gay,
Trip away
Round about your Queen !

Poor Elfie mourned their loss the most, and
would spend whole hours in looking upon the
rose that her playfellow had given her, and
singing over it the pretty airs she had taught
her; till at length when the year's charm had

passed away and it began to fade, she planted the stalk in her garden, and there it grew and grew till she could sit under the shade of it and think of her friend Gossamer.

THE SALAD.

As a merry young huntsman was once going briskly along through a wood, there came up a little old woman, and said to him " Good day, good day; you seem merry enough, but I am hungry and thirsty; do pray give me something to eat." The huntsman took pity on her, and put his hand in his pocket and gave her what he had. Then he wanted to go his way; but she took hold of him, and said " Listen, my friend, to what I am going to tell you; I will reward you for your kindness; go your way, and after a little time you will come to a tree where you will see nine birds sitting on a cloak. Shoot into the midst of them, and one will fall down dead: the cloak will fall too; take it, it is a wishing-cloak, and when you wear it you will find yourself at any place where you may wish to be. Cut open the dead bird, take out its heart and keep it, and you will find a piece of gold under your pillow every morning when you rise. It is the bird's heart that will bring you this good luck.

The huntsman thanked her, and thought to himself, " If all this does happen, it will be a fine thing for me." When he had gone a hundred steps or so, he heard a screaming and chirping in the branches over him, and looked up and saw a flock of birds pulling a cloak with their bills and feet; screaming, fighting, and tugging at each other as if each wished to have it himself. " Well," said the huntsman, " this is wonderful; this happens just as the old woman said; " then he shot into the midst of them so that their feathers flew all about. Off went the flock chattering away; but one fell down dead, and the cloak with it. Then the huntsman did as the old woman told him, cut open the bird, took out the heart, and carried the cloak home with him.

The next morning when he awoke he lifted up his pillow, and there lay the piece of gold glittering underneath; the same happened next day, and indeed every day when he arose. He heaped up a great deal of gold, and at last thought to himself, " Of what use is this gold to me whilst I am at home ? I will go out into the world and look about me."

Then he took leave of his friends, and hung his bag and bow about his neck, and went his way. It so happened that his road one day led through a thick wood, at the end of which was a large castle in a green meadow, and at one of the windows stood an old woman with a very beautiful young lady by her side looking about them. Now the old woman was a fairy, and said to the young lady, " There is a young man coming out of the wood who carries a wonderful prize; we must get it away from him, my dear child, for it is more fit for us than for him. He has a bird's heart that brings a piece of gold under his pillow every morning." Meantime the huntsman came nearer and looked at the lady, and said to himself, " I have been travelling so long that I should like to go into this castle and rest myself, for I have money enough to pay for any thing I want;" but the real reason was, that he wanted to see more of the beautiful lady. Then he went into the house, and was welcomed kindly; and it was not long before he was so much in love that he thought of nothing else but looking at the lady's eyes, and doing every thing that she wished. Then the old woman said, " Now is the time for getting the bird's heart." So the lady stole it away, and he never found any more gold under his pillow, for it lay now under the young lady's, and the old woman took it away every morning; but he was so much in love that he never missed his prize.

" Well," said the old fairy, " we have got the bird's heart, but not the wishing-cloak yet, and that we must also get." " Let us leave him that," said the young lady; " he has already lost his wealth." Then the fairy was very angry, and said, " Such a cloak is a very rare and wonderful thing, and I must

and will have it." So she did as the old woman told her, and set herself at the window,
and looked about the country and seemed
very sorrowful ; then the huntsman said,
" What makes you so sad ?" " Alas ! dear
sir," said she, " yonder lies the granite
rock where all the costly diamonds grow,
and I want so much to go there, that whenever I think of it I cannot help being sorrowful, for who can reach it ? only the birds
and the flies,—man cannot." " If that's all
your grief," said the huntsman, " I 'll take
you there with all my heart ;" so he drew
her under his cloak, and the moment he
wished to be on the granite mountain they
were both there. The diamonds glittered
so on all sides that they were delighted with
the sight and picked up the finest. But the
old fairy made a deep sleep come upon him,
and he said to the young lady, " Let us sit
down and rest ourselves a little, I am so
tired that I cannot stand any longer." So
they sat down, and he laid his head in her
lap and fell asleep; and whilst he was sleeping
on she took the cloak from his shoulders,

hung it on her own, picked up the diamonds, and wished herself home again.

When he awoke and found that his lady had tricked him, and left him alone on the wild rock, he said, " Alas! what roguery there is in the world!" and there he sat in great grief and fear, not knowing what to do. Now this rock belonged to fierce giants who lived upon it; and as he saw three of them striding about, he thought to himself, " I can only save myself by feigning to be asleep;" so he laid himself down as if he were in a sound sleep. When the giants came up to him, the first pushed him with his foot, and said, " What worm is this that lies here curled up?" " Tread upon him and kill him," said the second. " It's not worth the trouble," said the third; " let him live, he'll go climbing higher up the mountain, and some cloud will come rolling and carry him away." And they passed on. But the huntsman had heard all they said; and as soon as they were gone, he climbed to the top of the mountain, and when he had sat there a short time a cloud came rolling around him, and caught him in a whirlwind and bore him along for some time, till it settled in a garden, and he fell quite gently to the ground amongst the greens and cabbages.

Then he looked around him, and said, " I wish I had something to eat, if not I shall be worse off than before ; for here I see neither apples nor pears, nor any kind of fruits, nothing but vegetables." At last he thought to himself, " I can eat salad, it will refresh and strengthen me." So he picked out a fine head and ate of it ; but scarcely had he swallowed two bites when he felt himself quite changed, and saw with horror that he was turned into an ass. However, he still felt very hungry, and the salad tasted very nice ; so he ate on till he came to another kind of salad, and scarcely had he tasted it when he felt another change come over him, and soon saw that he was lucky enough to have found his old shape again.

Then he laid himself down and slept off a little of his weariness ; and when he awoke the next morning he broke off a head both of the good and the bad salad, and thought to himself,

" This will help me to my fortune again, and enable me to pay off some folks for their treachery. So he went away to try and find the castle of his old friends ; and after wandering about a few days he luckily found it. Then he stained his face all over brown, so that even his mother would not have known him, and went into the castle and asked for a lodging; " I am so tired," said he, " that I can go no further." " Countryman," said the fairy, " who are you ? and what is your business ? " " I am," said he, " a messenger sent by the king to find the finest salad that grows under the sun. I have been lucky enough to find it, and have brought it with me ; but the heat of the sun scorches so that it begins to wither, and I don't know that I can carry it further."

When the fairy and the young lady heard of this beautiful salad, they longed to taste it, and said, " Dear countryman, let us just taste it." " To be sure," answered he ; " I have two heads of it with me, and will give you one ;" so he opened his bag and gave them the bad. Then the fairy herself took it into the kitchen to be dressed ; and when it was ready she could not wait till it was carried up, but took a few leaves immediately and put them in her mouth, and scarcely were they swallowed when she lost her own form and ran braying down into the court in the form of an ass. Now the servant maid came into the kitchen, and seeing the salad ready was going to carry it up; but in the way she too felt a wish to taste it as the old woman had done, and ate some leaves; so she also was turned into an ass and ran after the other, letting the dish with the salad fall on the ground. The messenger sat all this time with the beautiful young lady, and as nobody came with the salad and she longed to taste it, she said, " I don't know where the salad can be." Then he thought something must have happened, and said, " I will go into the kitchen and see." And as he went he saw two asses in the court running about, and the salad lying on the ground. " All right!" said he; " those two have had their share." Then he took up the rest of the leaves, laid them on the dish and brought them to the young lady, saying, " I bring you the dish myself that you may not wait any longer." So she ate of it, and like the others ran off into the court, braying away.

Then the huntsman washed his face and went into the court that they might know him. "Now you shall be paid for your roguery," said he; and tied them all three to a rope and took them along with him till he came to a mill and knocked at the window. "What's the matter?" said the miller. "I have three tiresome beasts here," said the other; "if you will take them, give them food and room, and treat them as I tell you, I will pay you whatever you ask." "With all my heart," said the miller; "but how shall I treat them?" Then the huntsman said, "Give the old one stripes three times a day and hay once; give the next (who was the servant-maid) stripes once a day and hay three times; and give the youngest (who was the beautiful lady) hay three times a day and no stripes:" for he could not find it in his heart to have her beaten. After this he went back to the castle, where he found every thing he wanted.

Some days after the miller came to him

and told him that the old ass was dead;
" the other two," said he, " are alive and
eat, but are so sorrowful that they cannot
last long." Then the huntsman pitied them,
and told the miller to drive them back to him,
and when they came, he gave them some of
the good salad to eat. And the beautiful
young lady fell upon her knees before him,
and said, " O dearest huntsman! forgive
me all the ill I have done you; my mother forced me to it, it was against my
will, for I always loved you very much.
Your wishing-cloak hangs up in the closet,
and as for the bird's heart, I will give it you
too." But he said, " Keep it, it will be just
the same thing, for I mean to make you my
wife." So they were married, and lived together very happily till they died.

THE NOSE.

Dɪᴅ you ever hear the story of the three poor
soldiers, who, after having fought hard in the
wars, set out on their road home begging
their way as they went?

They had journeyed on a long way, sick
at heart with their bad luck at thus being
turned loose on the world in their old days,
when one evening they reached a deep
gloomy wood through which they must pass;
night came fast upon them, and they found
that they must, however unwillingly, sleep in
the wood; so to make all as safe as they could,
it was agreed that two should lie down and
sleep, while a third sat up and watched lest
wild beasts should break in and tear them
to pieces; when he was tired he was to wake
one of the others and sleep in his turn, and
so on with the third, so as to share the work
fairly among them.

The two who were to rest first soon lay
down and fell fast asleep, and the other made
himself a good fire under the trees and sat

down by the side to keep watch. He had not sat long before all on a sudden up came a little man in a red jacket. " Who 's there ? " said he. "A friend," said the soldier. "What sort of a friend?" " An old broken soldier," said the other, " with his two comrades who have nothing left to live on ; come, sit down and warm yourself." " Well, my worthy fellow," said the little man, " I will do what I can for you; take this and show it to your comrades in the morning. So he took out an old cloak and gave it to the soldier, telling him that whenever he put it over his shoulders any thing that he wished for would be fulfilled ; then the little man made him a bow and walked away.

The second soldier's turn to watch soon came, and the first laid himself down to sleep ; but the second man had not sat by himself long before up came the little man in the red jacket again. The soldier treated him in a friendly way as his comrade had done, and the little man gave him a purse, which he told him was always full of gold, let him draw as much as he would.

Then the third soldier's turn to watch came, and he also had the little man for his guest, who gave him a wonderful horn that drew crowds around it whenever it was played; and made every one forget his business to come and dance to its beautiful music.

In the morning each told his story and showed his treasure; and as they all liked each other very much and were old friends, they agreed to travel together to see the world, and for a while only to make use of the wonderful purse. And thus they spent their time very joyously, till at last they began to be tired of this roving life, and thought they should like to have a home of their own. So the first soldier put his old cloak on, and wished for a fine castle. In a moment it stood before their eyes; fine gardens and green lawns spread round it, and flocks of sheep and goats and herds of oxen were grazing about, and out of the gate came a fine coach with three dapple gray horses to meet them and bring them home.

All this was very well for a time; but it would not do to stay at home always, so they got together all their rich clothes and houses and servants, and ordered their coach with three horses, and set out on a journey to see a neighbouring king. Now this king had an only daughter, and as he took the three soldiers for kings' sons, he gave them a kind welcome. One day, as the second soldier was walking with the princess, she saw him with the wonderful purse in his hand; and having asked him what it was, he was foolish enough to tell her;—though indeed it did not much signify, for she was a witch and knew all the wonderful things that the three soldiers brought. Now this princess was very cunning and artful; so she set to work and made a purse so like the soldier's that no one would know one from the other, and then asked him to come and see her, and made him drink some wine that she had got ready for him, till he fell fast asleep. Then she felt in his pocket, and took away the wonderful purse and left the one she had made in its place.

The next morning the soldiers set out home, and soon after they reached their castle, happening to want some money, they went to their purse for it, and found something indeed in it, but to their great sorrow when they had emptied it, none came in the place of what they took. Then the cheat was soon found out; for the second soldier knew where he had been, and how he had told the story to the princess, and he guessed that she had betrayed him, "Alas!" cried he, "poor wretches that we are, what shall we do?" "Oh!" said the first soldier, "let no gray hairs grow for this mishap; I will soon get the purse back." So he threw his cloak across his shoulders and wished himself in the princess's chamber. There he found her sitting alone, telling her gold that fell around her in a shower from the purse. But the soldier stood looking at her too long, for the moment she saw him she started up and cried out with all her force, "Thieves! Thieves!" so that the whole court came running in and tried to seize him. The poor soldier now began to be dreadfully frightened in his turn, and thought it was high time to make the best of his way off; so without thinking of the ready way of travelling that his cloak gave him, he ran to the window, opened it, and jumped out; and unluckily in his haste his cloak caught and was left hanging, to the great joy of the princess, who knew its worth.

The poor soldier made the best of his way home to his comrades, on foot and in a very downcast mood; but the third soldier told him to keep up his heart, and took his horn and blew a merry tune. At the first blast a countless troop of foot and horse came rushing to their aid, and they set out to make war against their enemy. Then the king's palace was besieged, and he was told that he must give up the purse and cloak, or that not one stone should be left upon another. And the king went into his daughter's chamber and talked with her; but she said, " Let me try first if I cannot beat them some other way." So she thought of a cunning scheme to overreach them, and dressed herself out as a poor girl with a basket on her arm ; and set out by night with her maid, and went into the enemy's camp as if she wanted to sell trinkets.

In the morning she began to ramble about,

singing ballads so beautifully, that all the
tents were left empty, and the soldiers ran
round in crowds and thought of nothing but
hearing her sing. Amongst the rest came
the soldier to whom the horn belonged, and
as soon as she saw him she winked to her
maid, who slipped slily through the crowd and
went into his tent where it hung, and stole
it away. This done, they both got safely
back to the palace; the besieging army went
away, the three wonderful gifts were all left
in the hands of the princess, and the three soldiers were as pennyless and forlorn as when
the little man with the red jacket found them
in the wood.

Poor fellows! they began to think what
was now to be done. "Comrades," at last
said the second soldier, who had had the
purse, " we had better part, we cannot live
together, let each seek his bread as well
as he can." So he turned to the right,
and the other two to the left; for they said
they would rather travel together. Then on
he strayed till he came to a wood; (now this
was the same wood where they had met with

G Cruikshank fec

so much good luck before;) and he walked
on a long time till evening began to fall, when
he sat down tired beneath a tree, and soon
fell asleep.

Morning dawned, and he was greatly delighted, at opening his eyes, to see that the tree
was laden with the most beautiful apples. He
was hungry enough, so he soon plucked and
ate first one, then a second, then a third
apple. A strange feeling came over his nose:
when he put the apple to his mouth something was in the way; he felt it; it was his
nose, that grew and grew till it hung down to
his breast. It did not stop there, still it grew
and grew; " Heavens ! " thought he, " when
will it have done growing?" And well might
he ask, for by this time it reached the ground
as he sat on the grass, and thus it kept creeping
on till he could not bear its weight, or raise
himself up ; and it seemed as if it would never end, for already it stretched its enormous
length all through the wood.

Meantime his comrades were journeying
on, till on a sudden one of them stumbled
against something. " What can that be ? "

said the other. They looked, and could think of nothing that it was like but a nose. "We will follow it and find its owner, however," said they; so they traced it up till at last they found their poor comrade lying stretched along under the apple tree. What was to be done? They tried to carry him, but in vain. They caught an ass that was passing by, and raised him upon its back; but it was soon tired of carrying such a load. So they sat down in despair, when up came the little man in the red jacket. "Why, how now, friend?" said he, laughing; "well, I must find a cure for you, I see." So he told them to gather a pear from a tree that grew close by, and the nose would come right again. No time was lost, and the nose was soon brought to its proper size, to the poor soldier's joy.

"I will do something more for you yet," said the little man; "take some of those pears and apples with you; whoever eats one of the apples will have his nose grow like yours just now; but if you give him a pear, all will come right again. Go to the princess and get her to eat some of your apples; her nose will grow twenty times as long as yours did; then look sharp, and you will get what you want of her."

Then they thanked their old friend very heartily for all his kindness, and it was agreed that the poor soldier who had already tried the power of the apple should undertake the task. So he dressed himself up as a gardener's boy, and went to the king's palace, and said he had apples to sell, such as were never seen there before. Every one that saw them was delighted and wanted to taste, but he said they were only for the princess; and she soon sent her maid to buy his stock. They were so ripe and rosy that she soon began eating, and had already eaten three when she too began to wonder what ailed her nose, for it grew and grew, down to the ground, out at the window, and over the garden, nobody knows where.

Then the king made known to all his kingdom, that whoever would heal her of this dreadful disease should be richly rewarded. Many tried, but the princess got no relief. And now the old soldier dressed himself up very sprucely as a doctor, who said he could cure her; so he chopped up some of the apple, and to punish her a little more gave her a dose, saying he would call to-morrow and see her again. The morrow came, and of course, instead of being better, the nose had been growing fast all night, and the poor princess was in a dreadful fright. So the doctor chopped up a very little of the pear and gave her, and said he was sure that would do good, and he would call again the next day. Next day came, and the nose was to be sure a little smaller, but yet it was bigger than it was when the doctor first began to meddle with it.

Then he thought to himself, " I must frighten this cunning princess a little more before I shall get what I want of her;" so he gave her another dose of the apple, and said he would call on the morrow. The morrow came, and the nose was ten times as bad as before. " My good lady," said the doctor; " something works against my me-dicine, and is too strong for it; but I know by the force of my art what it is; you have stolen goods about you, I am sure, and if you do not give them back, I can do nothing for you." But the princess denied very stoutly that she had any thing of the kind. "Very well," said the doctor, "you may do as you please, but I am sure I am right, and you will die if you do not own it." Then he went to the king, and told him how the matter stood. "Daughter," said he, "send back the cloak, the ring, and the horn, that you stole from the right owners."

Then she ordered her maid to fetch all three, and gave them to the doctor, and begged him to give them back to the soldiers; and the moment he had them safe he gave her a whole pear to eat, and the nose came right. And as for the doctor, he put on the cloak, wished the king and all his court a good day, and was soon with his two brothers, who lived from that time happily at home in their palace, except when they took airings in their coach with the three dapple gray horses.

THE FIVE SERVANTS.

Some time ago there reigned in a country many thousands of miles off, an old queen who was very spiteful and delighted in nothing so much as mischief. She had one daughter, who was thought to be the most beautiful princess in the world; but her mother only made use of her as a trap for the unwary; and whenever any suitor who had heard of her beauty came to seek her in marriage, the only answer the old lady gave to each was, that he must undertake some very hard task and forfeit his life if he failed. Many, led by the report of the princess's charms, undertook these tasks, but failed in doing what the queen set them to do. No mercy was ever shown them; but the word was given at once, and off their heads were cut.

Now it happened that a prince who lived in a country far off, heard of the great beauty of this young lady, and said to his father, " Dear father, let me go and try my luck." " No," said the king; " if you go you will surely lose your life." The prince, however, had set his heart so much upon the scheme, that when he found his father was against it he fell very ill, and took to his bed for seven years, and no art could cure him, or recover his lost spirits : so when his father saw that if he went on thus he would die, he said to him with a heart full of grief, " If it must be so, go and try your luck." At this he rose from his bed, recovered his health and spirits, and went forward on his way light of heart and full of joy.

Then on he journeyed over hill and dale, through fair weather and foul, till one day, as he was riding through a wood, he thought he saw afar off some large animal upon the ground, and as he drew near he found that it was a man lying along upon the grass under the trees; but he looked more like a mountain than a man, he was so fat and jolly. When this big fellow saw the traveller, he arose, and said, " If you want any one to wait upon you, you will do well to take me into your service." " What should I do with such a fat fellow as you?" said the

prince. " It would be nothing to you if I
were three thousand times as fat," said the
man, " so that I do but behave myself well."
That 's true," answered the prince; " so
come with me, I can put you to some use or
another I dare say." Then the fat man rose
up and followed the prince, and by and by
they saw another man lying on the ground
with his ear close to the turf. The prince
said, " What are you doing there ?" " I
am listening," answered the man. " To
what ?" " To all that is going on in the
world, for I can hear every thing, I can even
hear the grass grow." " Tell me," said the
prince, " what you hear is going on at the
court of the old queen, who has the beautiful daughter ?" " I hear," said the listener,
" the noise of the sword that is cutting off
the head of one of her suitors." " Well !"
said the prince, " I see I shall be able to
make you of use ;—come along with me !"
They had not gone far before they saw a
pair of feet, and then part of the legs of a
man stretched out ; but they were so long
that they could not see the rest of the body,

till they had passed on a good deal further, and at last they came to the body, and, after going on a while further, to the head; "Bless me!" said the prince, "what a long rope you are!" "Oh!" answered the tall man, "this is nothing; when I choose to stretch myself to my full length, I am three times as high as any mountain you have seen on your travels, I warrant you; I will willingly do what I can to serve you if you will let me." "Come along then," said the prince, "I can turn you to account in some way."

The prince and his train went on further into the wood, and next saw a man lying by the road side basking in the heat of the sun, yet shaking and shivering all over, so that not a limb lay still. "What makes you shiver," said the king, "while the sun is shining so warm?" "Alas!" answered the man, "the warmer it is, the colder I am; the sun only seems to me like a sharp frost that thrills through all my bones; and on the other hand, when others are what you call cold I begin to be warm, so that I can neither bear the ice for its heat nor the fire for its cold."

" You are a queer fellow," said the prince ;
" but if you have nothing else to do, come
along with me." The next thing they saw was
a man standing, stretching his neck and looking around him from hill to hill. " What
are you looking for so eagerly ?" said the
prince. " I have such sharp eyes," said the
man, " that I can see over woods and fields
and hills and dales ;—in short, all over the
world." " Well," said the prince, " come
with me if you will, for I want one more to
make up my train."

Then they all journeyed on, and met with
no one else till they came to the city where the
beautiful princess lived. The prince went
straight to the old queen, and said, " Here I
am, ready to do any task you set me, if you will
give me your daughter as a reward when I have
done." " I will set you three tasks," said the
queen ; " and if you get through all, you shall
be the husband of my daughter. First, you
must bring me a ring which I dropped in the
red sea." The prince went home to his
friends and said, " The first task is not an
easy one ; it is to fetch a ring out of the red

sea, so lay your heads together and say what is to be done." Then the sharp-sighted one said, " I will see where it lies," and looked down into the sea, and cried out, " There it lies upon a rock at the bottom." " I would fetch it out," said the tall man, " if I could but see it." " Well!" cried out the fat one, " I will help you to do that," and laid himself down and held his mouth to the water, and drank up the waves till the bottom of the sea was as dry as a meadow. Then the tall man stooped a little and pulled out the ring with his hand, and the prince took it to the old queen, who looked at it, and wondering said, " It is indeed the right ring; you have gone through this task well: but now comes the second; look yonder at the meadow before my palace; see! there are a hundred fat oxen feeding there; you must eat them all up before noon : and underneath in my cellar there are a hundred casks of wine, which you must drink all up." " May I not invite some guests to share the feast with me?" said the prince. " Why, yes!" said the old woman with a spiteful laugh;

" you may ask one of your friends to break-fast with you, but no more.

Then the prince went home and said to the fat man, " You must be my guest to-day, and for once you shall eat your fill." So the fat man set to work and ate the hundred oxen without leaving a bit, and asked if that was to be all he should have for his breakfast ? and he drank the wine out of the casks without leaving a drop, licking even his fingers when he had done. When the meal was ended, the prince went to the old woman and told her the second task was done. " Your work is not all over, however," muttered the old hag to herself; " I will catch you yet, you shall not keep your head upon your shoulders if I can help it." " This evening," said she, " I will bring my daughter into your house and leave her with you; you shall sit together there, but take care that you do not fall asleep; for I shall come when the clock strikes twelve, and if she is not then with you, you are undone." " O ! " thought the prince, " it is an easy task to keep such a watch as that ; I will take care to keep my eyes open."

So he called his servants and told them all
that the old woman had said. " Who knows
though," said he, " but there may be some
trick at the bottom of this ? it is as well to be
upon our guard and keep watch that the
young lady does not get away." When it
was night the old woman brought her daughter to the prince's house ; then the tall man
twisted himself round about it, the listener
put his ear to the ground, the fat man placed
himself before the door so that no living soul
could enter, and the sharp-eyed one looked
out afar and watched. Within sat the princess
without saying a word, but the moon shone
bright through the window upon her face, and
the prince gazed upon her wonderful beauty.
And while he looked upon her with a heart
full of joy and love, his eyelids did not droop ;
but at eleven o'clock the old woman cast a
charm over them so that they all fell asleep,
and the princess vanished in a moment.

And thus they slept till a quarter to twelve,
when the charm had no longer any power
over them, and they all awoke. " Alas !
alas ! woe is me," cried the prince ; " now I

am lost for ever." And his faithful servants began to weep over their unhappy lot; but the listener said, "Be still and I will listen;" so he listened a while, and cried out, "I hear her bewailing her fate;" and the sharp-sighted man looked, and said, "I see her sitting on a rock three hundred miles hence; now help us, my tall friend; if you stand up, you will reach her in two steps." "Very well," answered the tall man; and in an instant, before one could turn one's head round, he was at the foot of the enchanted rock. Then the tall man took the young lady in his arms and carried her back to the prince a moment before it struck twelve; and they all sat down again and made merry. And when the clock struck twelve the old queen came sneaking by with a spiteful look, as if she was going to say "Now he is mine;" nor could she think otherwise, for she knew that her daughter was but the moment before on the rock three hundred miles off; but when she came and saw her daughter in the prince's room, she started, and said "There is somebody here who can do more than I

can." However, she now saw that she could
no longer avoid giving the prince her daughter for a wife, but said to her in a whisper,
" It is a shame that you should be won by
servants, and not have a husband of your
own choice."

Now the young lady was of a very proud
haughty temper, and her anger was raised to
such a pitch, that the next morning she ordered three hundred loads of wood to be
brought and piled up; and told the prince it
was true he had by the help of his servants
done the three tasks, but that before she
would marry him some one must sit upon
that pile of wood when it was set on fire and
bear the heat. She thought to herself that
though his servants had done every thing else
for him, none of them would go so far as to
burn themselves for him, and that then she
should put his love to the test by seeing
whether he would sit upon it himself. But
she was mistaken; for when the servants
heard this, they said, " We have all done
something but the frosty man; now his turn
is come;" and they took him and put him

on the wood and set it on fire. Then the fire rose and burnt for three long days, till all the wood was gone; and when it was out, the frosty man stood in the midst of the ashes trembling like an aspen-leaf, and said, " I never shivered so much in my life; if it had lasted much longer, I should have lost the use of my limbs."

When the princess had no longer any plea for delay, she saw that she was bound to marry the prince; but when they were going to church, the old woman said, " I will never consent;" and sent secret orders out to her horsemen to kill and slay all before them and bring back her daughter before she could be married. However, the listener had pricked up his ears and heard all that the old woman said, and told it to the prince. So they made haste and got to the church first, and were married; and then the five servants took their leave and went away saying, " We will go and try our luck in the world on our own account."

The prince set out with his wife, and at the end of the first day's journey came to a village, where a swineherd was feeding his swine; and as they came near he said to his wife, " Do you know who I am ? I am not a prince, but a poor swineherd; he whom you see yonder with the swine is my father, and our business will be to help him to tend them." Then he went into the swineherd's hut with her, and ordered her royal clothes to be taken away in the night ; so that when she awoke in the morning, she had nothing to put on, till the woman who lived there made a great favour of giving her an old gown and a pair of worsted stockings. " If it were not for your husband's sake," said she, " I would not have given you any thing." Then the poor princess gave herself up for lost, and believed that her husband must indeed be a swineherd; but she thought she would make the best of it, and began to help him to feed them, and said, " It is a just reward for my pride." When this had lasted eight days she could bear it no longer, for her feet were all over wounds, and as she sat down and wept by the way-side, some people came up to her and pitied her, and asked if she knew what her husband really was. "Yes," said she; "a swineherd; he is just gone out to market with some of his stock." But they said, "Come along and we will take you to him;" and they took her over the hill to the palace of the prince's father; and when they came into the hall, there stood her husband so richly drest in his royal clothes that she did not know him till he fell upon her neck and kissed her, and said, "I have borne much for your sake, and you too have also borne a great deal for me." Then the guests were sent for, and the marriage feast was given, and all made merry and danced and sung, and the best wish that I can wish is, that you and I had been there too.

CAT-SKIN.

THERE was once a king, whose queen had hair of the purest gold, and was so beautiful that her match was not to be met with on the whole face of the earth. But this beautiful queen fell ill, and when she felt that her end drew near, she called the king to her and said, "Vow to me that you will never marry again, unless you meet with a wife who is as beautiful as I am, and who has golden hair like mine." Then when the king in his grief had vowed all she asked, she shut her eyes and died. But the king was not to be comforted, and for a long time never thought of taking another wife. At last, however, his counsellors said, "This will not do; the king must marry again, that we may have a queen." So messengers were sent far and wide, to seek for a bride who was as beautiful as the late queen. But there was no princess in the world so beautiful; and if there had been, still there was not one to be found who had such golden hair. So the messengers came

home and had done all their work for nothing.

Now the king had a daughter who was just
as beautiful as her mother, and had the same
golden hair.   And when she was grown
up, the king looked at her and saw that she
was just like his late queen: then he said to
his courtiers, " May I not marry my daughter ? she is the very image of my dead wife :
unless I have her, I shall not find any bride
upon the whole earth, and you say there
must be a queen."   When the courtiers
heard this, they were shocked, and said,
" Heaven forbid that a father should marry
his daughter ! out of so great a sin no good
can come."   And his daughter was also
shocked, but hoped the king would soon
give up such thoughts: so she said to him,
" Before I marry any one I must have three
dresses ; one must be of gold like the sun,
another must be of shining silver like the
moon, and a third must be dazzling as the
stars : besides this, I want a mantle of a
thousand different kinds of fur put together,
to which every beast in the kingdom must

give a part of his skin." And thus she
thought he would think of the matter no
more. But the king made the most skilful
workmen in his kingdom weave the three
dresses, one as golden as the sun, another as
silvery as the moon, and a third shining like
the stars; and his hunters were told to hunt
out all the beasts in his kingdom and take the
finest fur out of their skins : and so a mantle
of a thousand furs was made.

When all was ready, the king sent them
to her; but she got up in the night when all
were asleep, and took three of her trinkets,
a golden ring, a golden necklace, and a
golden broach ; and packed the three dresses
of the sun, moon, and stars, up in a nut-
shell, and wrapped herself up in the mantle
of all sorts of fur, and besmeared her face and
hands with soot. Then she threw herself
upon heaven for help in her need, and went
away and journeyed on the whole night, till
at last she came to a large wood. As she was
very tired, she sat herself down in the hollow of a tree and soon fell asleep : and there
she slept on till it was mid-day : and it hap-

pened, that as the king to whom the wood belonged was hunting in it, his dogs came to the tree, and began to snuff about and run round and round, and then to bark. " Look sharp," said the king to the huntsmen, " and see what sort of game lies there." And the huntsmen went up to the tree, and when they came back again said, " In the hollow tree there lies a most wonderful beast, such as we never saw before ; its skin seems of a thousand kinds of fur, but there it lies fast asleep. " See," said the king, "if you can catch it alive, and we will take it with us." So the huntsmen took it up, and the maiden awoke and was greatly frightened, and said "I am a poor child that has neither father nor mother left ; have pity on me and take me with you." Then they said, " Yes, Miss Cat-skin, you will do for the kitchen ; you can sweep up the ashes and do things of that sort." So they put her in the coach and took her home to the king's palace. Then they showed her a little corner under the staircase where no light of day ever peeped in, and said, " Cat-skin, you may lie and sleep there." And she was sent into the kitchen, and made to fetch wood and water, to blow the fire, pluck the poultry, pick the herbs, sift the ashes, and do all the dirty work.

Thus Cat-skin lived for a long time very sorrowfully. "Ah! pretty princess!" thought she, "what will now become of thee?" But it happened one day that a feast was to be held in the king's castle; so she said to the cook, "May I go up a little while and see what is going on? I will take care and stand behind the door." And the cook said, "Yes, you may go, but be back again in half an hour's time to rake out the ashes." Then she took her little lamp, and went into her cabin, and took off the fur skin, and washed the soot from off her face and hands, so that her beauty shone forth like the sun from behind the clouds. She next opened her nutshell, and brought out of it the dress that shone like the sun, and so went to the feast. Every one made way for her, for nobody knew her, and they thought she could be no less than a king's daughter. But the king came up to her and held out his hand and danced with her, and he thought in his heart, "I never saw any one half so beautiful."

When the dance was at an end, she curtsied; and when the king looked round for her, she was gone, no one knew whither. The guards who stood at the castle gate were called in; but they had seen no one. The truth was, that she had run into her little cabin, pulled off her dress, blacked her face and hands, put on the fur-skin cloak, and was Cat-skin again. When she went into the kitchen to her work, and began to rake the ashes, the cook said, "Let that alone till the morning, and heat the king's soup; I should like to run up now and give a peep; but take care you don't let a hair fall into it, or you will run a chance of never eating again."

As soon as the cook went away, Cat-skin heated the king's soup and toasted up a slice of bread as nicely as ever she could; and when it was ready, she went and looked in the cabin for her little golden ring, and put it into the dish in which the soup was. When the dance was over, the king ordered

his soup to be brought in, and it pleased him
so well, that he thought he had never tasted
any so good before. At the bottom he saw
a gold ring lying, and as he could not make
out how it had got there, he ordered the cook
to be sent for. The cook was frightened when
he heard the order, and said to Cat-skin,
" You must have let a hair fall into the soup;
if it be so, you will have a good beating."
Then she went before the king, and he asked
her who had cooked the soup. "I did," answered she. But the king said, " That is not
true; it was better done than you could do it."
Then she answered, "To tell the truth, I did
not cook it, but Cat-skin did." " Then let
Cat-skin come up," said the king: and when
she came, he said to her, " Who are you?"
" I am a poor child," said she, "who has lost
both father and mother." "How came you
in my palace?" asked he. " I am good for
nothing," said she, "but to be scullion girl,
and to have boots and shoes thrown at my
head." " But how did you get the ring that
was in the soup?" asked the king. But she
would not own that she knew any thing about

K 2

the ring; so the king sent her away again about her business.

After a time there was another feast, and Cat-skin asked the cook to let her go up and see it as before. " Yes," said he, "but come back again in half an hour, and cook the king the soup that he likes so much." Then she ran to her little cabin, washed herself quickly, and took the dress out which was silvery as the moon, and put it on; and when she went in looking like a king's daughter, the king went up to her and rejoiced at seeing her again, and when the dance began, he danced with her. After the dance was at an end, she managed to slip out so slily that the king did not see where she was gone; but she sprang into her little cabin and made herself into Cat-skin again, and went into the kitchen to cook the soup. Whilst the cook was above, she got the golden necklace, and dropped it into the soup; then it was brought to the king, who ate it, and it pleased him as well as before; so he sent for the cook, who was again forced to tell him that Cat-skin had cooked it. Cat-skin was brought

again before the king; but she still told him
that she was only fit to have the boots and
shoes thrown at her head.

But when the king had ordered a feast to
be got ready for the third time, it happened
just the same as before. "You must be a
witch, Cat-skin," said the cook; "for you
always put something into the soup, so that
it pleases the king better than mine." However, he let her go up as before. Then she
put on the dress which sparkled like the stars,
and went into the ball-room in it; and the
king danced with her again, and thought she
had never looked so beautiful as she did then:
so whilst he was dancing with her, he put a
gold ring on her finger without her seeing it,
and ordered that the dance should be kept up
a long time. When it was at an end, he would
have held her fast by the hand; but she slipt
away and sprang so quickly through the
crowd that he lost sight of her; and she ran
as fast as she could into her little cabin under
the stairs. But this time she kept away too
long, and staid beyond the half-hour; so she
had not time to take off her fine dress, but

threw her fur mantle over it, and in her haste did not soot herself all over, but left one finger white.

Then she ran into the kitchen, and cooked the king's soup; and as soon as the cook was gone, she put the golden broach into the dish. When the king got to the bottom, he ordered Cat-skin to be called once more, and soon saw the white finger and the ring that he had put on it whilst they were dancing: so he seized her hand, and kept fast hold of it, and when she wanted to loose herself and spring away, the fur cloak fell off a little on one side, and the starry dress sparkled underneath it. Then he got hold of the fur and tore it off, and her golden hair and beautiful form were seen, and she could no longer hide herself: so she washed the soot and ashes from off her face, and showed herself to be the most beautiful princess upon the face of the earth. But the king said, "You are my beloved bride, and we will never more be parted from each other." And the wedding feast was held, and a merry day it was.

THE ROBBER-BRIDEGROOM.

THERE was once a miller who had a pretty daughter; and when she was grown up, he thought to himself, "If a seemly man should come to ask her for his wife, I will give her to him that she may be taken care of." Now it so happened that one did come, who seemed to be very rich, and behaved very well; and as the miller saw no reason to find fault with him, he said he should have his daughter. Yet the maiden did not love him quite so well as a bride ought to love her bridegroom, but, on the other hand, soon began to feel a kind of inward shuddering whenever she saw or thought of him.

One day he said to her, "Why do you not come and see my home, since you are to be my bride?" "I do not know where your house is," said the girl. "'Tis out there," said her bridegroom, "yonder in the dark green wood." Then she began to try and avoid going, and said, "But I cannot find the way thither." "Well, but you must come

and see me next Sunday," said the bridegroom; "I have asked some guests to meet
you, and that you may find your way through
the wood, I will strew ashes for you along
the path."

When Sunday came and the maiden was
to go out, she felt very much troubled, and
took care to put on two pockets, and filled
them with peas and beans. She soon came
to the wood, and found her path strewed with
ashes; so she followed the track, and at every
step threw a pea on the right and a bean on
the left side of the road; and thus she journeyed on the whole day till she came to a
house which stood in the middle of the dark
wood. She saw no one within, and all was quite
still, till on a sudden she heard a voice cry,

> "Turn again, bonny bride!
> Turn again home !
> Haste from the robber's den,
> Haste away home !"

She looked around, and saw a little bird sitting in a cage that hung over the door; and
he flapped his wings, and again she heard
him cry,

"Turn again, bonny bride!
Turn again home!
Haste from the robber's den,
Haste away home!"

However, the bride went in, and roamed along from one room to another, and so over all the house; but it was quite empty, and not a soul could she see. At last she came to a room where a very very old woman was sitting. "Pray, can you tell me, my good woman," said she, "if my bridegroom lives here?" "Ah! my dear child!" said the old woman, "you are come to fall into the trap laid for you: your wedding can only be with Death, for the robber will surely take away your life; if I do not save you, you are lost!" So she hid the bride behind a large cask, and then said to her, "Do not stir or move yourself at all, lest some harm should befall you; and when the robbers are asleep we will run off; I have long wished to get away."

She had hardly done this when the robbers came in, and brought another young maiden with them that had been ensnared like the bride. Then they began to feast and

K 5

drink, and were deaf to her shrieks and groans: and they gave her some wine to drink, three glasses, one of white, one of red, and one of yellow; upon which she fainted and fell down dead. Now the bride began to grow very uneasy behind the cask, and thought that she too must die in her turn. Then the one that was to be her bridegroom saw that there was a gold ring on the little finger of the maiden they had murdered; and as he tried to snatch it off, it flew up in the air and fell down again behind the cask just in the bride's lap. So he took a light and searched about all round the room for it, but could not find any thing; and another of the robbers said, "Have you looked behind the large cask yet?" "Pshaw!" said the old woman, "come, sit still and eat your supper now, and leave the ring alone till to-morrow; it won't run away, I'll warrant."

So the robbers gave up the search, and went on with their eating and drinking; but the old woman dropped a sleeping-draught into their wine, and they laid themselves down and slept, and snored roundly. And when

the bride heard this, she stepped out from behind the cask; and as she was forced to walk
over the sleepers, who were lying about on
the floor, she trembled lest she should awaken
some of them. But heaven aided her, so that
she soon got through her danger; and the old
woman went up stairs with her, and they
both ran away from this murderous den.
The ashes that had been strewed were now
all blown away, but the peas and beans
had taken root and were springing up, and
showed her the way by the light of the moon.
So they walked the whole night, and in the
morning reached the mill; when the bride
told her father all that had happened to her.

As soon as the day arrived when the wedding was to take place, the bridegroom came;
and the miller gave orders that all his friends
and relations should be asked to the feast.
And as they were all sitting at table, one of
them proposed that each of the guests should
tell some tale.   Then the bridegroom said to
the bride, when it came to her turn, " Well,
my dear, do you know nothing? come, tell us
some story." " Yes," answered she, " I can

tell you a dream that I dreamt. I once thought I was going through a wood, and went on and on till I came to a house where there was not a soul to be seen, but a bird in a cage, that cried out twice,

> "Turn again, bonny bride!
> Turn again home!
> Haste from the robber's den,
> Haste away home!"

—I only dreamt that, my love. Then I went through all the rooms, which were quite empty, until I came to a room where there sat a very old woman; and I said to her, 'Does my bridegroom live here?' but she answered, 'Ah! my dear child! you have fallen into a murderer's snare; your bridegroom will surely kill you;'—I only dreamt that, my love. But she hid me behind a large cask; and hardly had she done this, when the robbers came in, dragging a young woman along with them; then they gave her three kinds of wine to drink, white, red, and yellow, till she fell dead upon the ground;—I only dreamt that, my love. After they had done this, one of the robbers saw that there was a gold ring

on her little finger, and snatched at it; but it
flew up to the ceiling, and then fell behind the
great cask just where I was, and into my lap;
and here is the ring!" At these words she
brought out the ring and showed it to the
guests.

When the robber saw all this, and heard
what she said, he grew as pale as ashes with
fright, and wanted to run off; but the guests
held him fast and gave him up to justice, so
that he and all his gang met with the due reward of their wickedness.

THE THREE SLUGGARDS.

THE king of a country a long way off had
three sons. He liked one as well as another,
and did not know which to leave his kingdom
to after his death: so when he was dying
he called them all to him, and said, " Dear
children, the laziest sluggard of the three
shall be king after me." " Then," said the
eldest, " the kingdom is mine; for I am so lazy
that when I lie down to sleep, if any thing

were to fall into my eyes so that I could not shut them, I should still go on sleeping." The second said, " Father, the kingdom belongs to me; for I am so lazy that when I sit by the fire to warm myself, I would sooner have my toes burnt than take the trouble to draw my legs back." The third said, " Father, the kingdom is mine; for I am so lazy that if I were going to be hanged, with the rope round my neck, and somebody were to put a sharp knife into my hands to cut it, I had rather be hanged than raise my hand to do it." When the father heard this, he said, " You shall be the king; for you are the fittest man."

THE SEVEN RAVENS.

There was once a man who had seven sons, and last of all one daughter. Although the little girl was very pretty, she was so weak and small that they thought she could not live; but they said she should at once be christened. So the father sent one of his sons in haste to the spring to get some water, but the other six ran with him. Each wanted to be first at drawing the water, and so they were in such a hurry that all let their pitchers fall into the well, and they stood very foolishly looking at one another, and did not know what to do, for none dared go home. In the mean time the father was uneasy, and could not tell what made the young men stay so long. "Surely," said he, "the whole seven must have forgotten themselves over some game of play;" and when he had waited still longer and they yet did not come, he flew into a rage and wished them all turned into ravens. Scarcely had he spoken these words when he heard a croaking over his head, and looked up and saw seven ravens as black as coals flying round and round. Sorry as he was to see his wish so fulfilled, he did not know how what was done could be undone, and comforted himself as well as he could for the loss of his seven sons with his dear little daughter, who soon became stronger and every day more beautiful.

For a long time she did not know that she

had ever had any brothers; for her father and mother took care not to speak of them before her: but one day by chance she heard the people about her speak of them. "Yes," said they, "she is beautiful indeed, but still 'tis a pity that her brothers should have been lost for her sake." Then she was much grieved, and went to her father and mother, and asked if she had any brothers, and what had become of them. So they dared no longer hide the truth from her, but said it was the will of heaven, and that her birth was only the innocent cause of it; but the little girl mourned sadly about it every day, and thought herself bound to do all she could to bring her brothers back; and she had neither rest nor ease, till at length one day she stole away, and set out into the wide world to find her brothers, wherever they might be, and free them, whatever it might cost her.

She took nothing with her but a little ring which her father and mother had given her, a loaf of bread in case she should be hungry, a little pitcher of water in case she should be thirsty, and a little stool to rest upon when she should be weary. Thus she went on and on, and journeyed till she came to the world's end: then she came to the sun, but the sun looked much too hot and fiery; so she ran away quickly to the moon, but the moon was cold and chilly, and said, " I smell flesh and blood this way!" so she took herself away in a hurry and came to the stars, and the stars were friendly and kind to her, and each star sat upon his own little stool; but the morning-star rose up and gave her a little piece of wood, and said, " If you have not this little piece of wood, you cannot unlock the castle that stands on the glass-mountain, and there your brothers live." The little girl took the piece of wood, rolled it up in a little cloth, and went on again until she came to the glass-mountain, and found the door shut. Then she felt for the little piece of wood; but when she unwrapped the cloth it was not there, and she saw she had lost the gift of the good stars. What was to be done? she wanted to save her brothers, and had no key of the castle of the glass-mountain; so this faithful little sister took a knife out of her pocket and cut off her little finger, that was just the size of the piece of wood she had lost, and put it in the door and opened it.

As she went in, a little dwarf came up to her, and said, " What are you seeking for ?" " I seek for my brothers, the seven ravens," answered she. Then the dwarf said, " My masters are not at home; but if you will wait till they come, pray step in." Now the little dwarf was getting their dinner ready, and he brought their food upon seven little plates, and their drink in seven little glasses, and set them upon the table, and out of each little plate their sister ate a small piece, and out of each little glass she drank a small drop; but she let the ring that she had brought with her fall into the last glass.

On a sudden she heard a fluttering and croaking in the air, and the dwarf said, " Here come my masters." When they came in, they wanted to eat and drink, and looked for their little plates and glasses. Then said one after the other, " Who has eaten from my little plate ? and who has been drinking out of my little glass ?

> " Caw ! Caw ! well I ween
> Mortal lips have this way been."

When the seventh came to the bottom of his glass, and found there the ring, he looked at it, and knew that it was his father's and mother's, and said, " O that our little sister would but come ! then we should be free." When the little girl heard this, (for she stood behind the door all the time and listened,) she ran forward, and in an instant all the ravens took their right form again ; and all hugged and kissed each other, and went merrily home.

ROLAND AND MAY-BIRD.

THERE was once a poor man who went every day to cut wood in the forest. One day as he went along he heard a cry like a little child's ; so he followed the sound till at last he looked up a high tree, and on one of the branches sat a very little girl. Its mother had fallen asleep, and a vulture had taken it out of her lap and flown away with it and left it on the tree. Then the wood-cutter climbed up, took the little child down, and said to himself, " I will take this poor child home and bring it up with my own son Roland." So he brought it to his cottage, and both grew up together; and he called the little girl May-bird, because he had found her on a tree in May; and May-bird and Roland were so very fond of each other that they were never happy but when they were together.

But the wood-cutter became very poor, and had nothing in the world he could call his own, and indeed he had scarcely bread enough for his wife and the two children to eat. At last the time came when even that was all gone, and he knew not where to seek for help in his need. Then at night, as he lay on his bed and turned himself here and there, restless and full of care, his wife said to him, " Husband, listen to me, and take the two children out early to-morrow morning; give each of them a piece of bread, and then lead them into the midst of the wood where it is thickest, make a fire for them, and go away and leave them alone to shift for themselves, for we can no longer keep them here." " No, wife," said the husband, " I cannot find it in my heart to leave the children to the wild beasts of the forest, who would soon tear them to pieces." " Well, if you will not do as I say," answered the wife, " we must all starve together: " and she let him have no peace until he came into her plan.

Meantime the poor children too were lying awake restless, and weak from hunger, so that they heard all that their mother said to her husband. " Now," thought May-bird to herself, " it is all up with us:" and she began to weep. But Roland crept to her bed-side, and said, " Do not be afraid, May-bird, I will find out some help for us." Then he got up, put on his jacket, and opened the door and went out.

The moon shone bright upon the little court before the cottage, and the white pebbles glittered like daisies on the green meadows. So he stooped down, and put as many as he could into his pocket, and then went back to the house. " Now, May-bird," said he, " rest in peace;" and he went to bed and fell fast asleep.

Early in the morning, before the sun had risen, the woodman's wife came and awoke them. " Get up, children," said she, " we are going into the wood; there is a piece of bread for each of you, but take care of it and keep some for the afternoon." May-bird took the bread and carried it in her apron, because Roland had his pocket full of stones, and they made their way into the wood.

After they had walked on for a time, Roland stood still and looked towards home, and after a while turned again, and so on several times. Then his father said, " Roland, why do you keep turning and lagging about so? move your legs on a little faster." " Ah ! father," answered Roland, " I am stopping to look at my white cat that sits on the roof, and wants to say good bye to me." " You little fool ! " said his mother, " that is not your cat; 'tis the morning sun shining on the chimney top." Now Roland had not been looking at the cat, but had all the while been staying behind to drop from his pocket one white pebble after another along the road.

When they came into the midst of the wood, the woodman said, " Run about, children, and pick up some wood, and I will make a fire to keep us all warm." So they piled up a litttle heap of brush-wood, and set it a-fire; and as the flame burnt bright, the mother said, " Now set yourselves by the fire and go to sleep, while we go and cut wood in the forest; be sure you wait till we come again and fetch you." Roland and May-bird sat by the fire-side till the after-noon, and then each of them ate their piece of bread. They fancied the woodman was still in the wood, because they thought they heard the blows of his axe; but it was a bough which he had cunningly hung upon a tree, so that the wind blew it backwards and forwards, and it sounded like the axe as it hit the other boughs. Thus they waited till evening; but the woodman and his wife kept away, and no one came to fetch them.

When it was quite dark May-bird began to cry; but Roland said, " Wait awhile till the moon rises." And when the moon rose, he took her by the hand, and there lay the pebbles along the ground, glittering like new pieces of money, and marked the way out. Towards morning they came again to the woodman's house, and he was glad in his heart when he saw the children again; for he had grieved at leaving them alone. His wife also seemed to be glad; but in her heart she was angry at it.

Not long after there was again no bread in the house, and May-bird and Roland heard the wife say to her husband, " The children found their way back once, and I took it in good part; but there is only half a loaf of bread left for them in the house; tomorrow you must take them deeper into the wood, that they may not find their way out, or we shall all be starved." It grieved the husband in his heart to do as his wife wished, and he thought it would be better to share their last morsel with the children; but as he had done as she said once, he did not dare to say no. When the children had heard all their plan, Roland got up and wanted to pick up pebbles as before; but when he came to the door he found his mother had locked it. Still he comforted May-bird, and said, " Sleep in peace, dear May-bird ; God is very kind and will help us." Early in the morning a piece of bread was given to each of them, but still smaller than the one they had before. Upon the road Roland crumbled his in his pocket, and often stood still, and threw a crumb upon the ground. " Why do you lag so behind, Roland?" said the woodman; " go your ways on before." " I am looking at my little dove that is sitting upon the roof and wants to say good bye to me." " You silly boy!" said the wife, " that is not your little dove, it is the morning sun that shines on the chimney top." But Roland went on crumbling his bread, and throwing it on the ground. And thus they went on still further into the wood, where they had never been before in all their life. There they were again told to sit down by a large fire, and sleep; and the wood-man and his wife said they would come in the

evening and fetch them away. In the afternoon Roland shared May-bird's bread, because he had strewed all his upon the road;
but the day passed away, and evening passed
away too, and no one came to the poor children. Still Roland comforted May-bird, and
said, " Wait till the moon rises; then I shall
see the crumbs of bread which I have strewed,
and they will show us the way home."

The moon rose; but when Roland looked
for the crumbs, they were gone; for thousands of little birds in the wood had found
them and picked them up. Roland, however,
set out to try and find his way home; but
they soon lost themselves in the wilderness,
and went on through the night and all the
next day, till at last they lay down and fell
asleep for weariness: and another day they
went on as before, but still did not reach
the end of the wood, and were as hungry as
could be, for they had nothing to eat.

In the afternoon of the third day they
came to a strange little hut, made of bread,
with a roof of cake, and windows of sparkling sugar. " Now we will sit down and

eat till we have had enough," said Roland;
" I will eat off the roof for my share; do you
eat the windows, May-bird, they will be
nice and sweet for you." Whilst May-bird,
however, was picking at the sugar, a sweet
pretty voice called from within;

  " Tip, tap! who goes there?"
But the children answered;

  " The wind, the wind,
   That blows through the air;"

and went on eating; and May-bird broke out
a round pane of the window for herself, and
Roland tore off a large piece of cake from the
roof, when the door opened, and a little old
fairy came gliding out. At this May-bird
and Roland were so frightened, that they
let fall what they had in their hands. But
the old lady shook her head, and said,
" Dear children, where have you been wandering about? come in with me; you shall
have something good." So she took them
both by the hand, and led them into her
little hut, and brought out plenty to eat,—
milk and pancakes, with sugar, apples, and
nuts; and then two beautiful little beds were

got ready, and May-bird and Roland laid themselves down, and thought they were in heaven: but the fairy was a spiteful one, and had made her pretty sweetmeat house to entrap little children. Early in the morning, before they were awake, she went to their little bed, and when she saw the two sleeping and looking so sweetly, she had no pity on them, but was glad they were in her power. Then she took up Roland, and put him in a little coop by himself; and when he awoke, he found himself behind a grating, shut up as little chickens are: but she shook May-bird, and called out, " Get up, you lazy little thing, and fetch some water; and go into the kitchen and cook something good to eat: your brother is shut up yonder; I shall first fatten him, and when he is fat, I think I shall eat him."

When the fairy was gone, the little girl watched her time and got up and ran to Roland, and told him what she had heard, and said, " We must run away quickly, for the old woman is a bad fairy, and will kill us." But Roland said, " You must first steal away her fairy wand, that we may save ourselves, if she should follow." Then the little maiden ran back and fetched the magic wand, and away they went together; so when the old fairy came back, she could see no one at home, and sprang in a great rage to the window, and looked out into the wide world, (which she could do far and near,) and a long way off she spied May-bird running away with her dear Roland; " You are already a great way off," said she; " but you will still fall into my hands." Then she put on her boots, which walked several miles at a step, and scarcely made two steps with them, before she overtook the children: but May-bird saw that the fairy was coming after them, and by the help of the wand turned her dear Roland into a lake, and herself into a swan which swam about in the middle of it. So the fairy set herself down on the shore, and took a great deal of trouble to decoy the swan, and threw crumbs of bread to it; but it would not come near her, and she was forced to go home in the evening, without taking her revenge. And May-bird changed herself and her dear Roland back into their own forms once more, and they went journeying on the whole night until the dawn of day; and then the maiden turned herself into a beautiful rose, which grew in the midst of a quickset hedge, and Roland sat by the side and played upon his flute.

The fairy soon came striding along. "Good piper," said she, "may I pluck the beautiful rose for myself?" "O yes," answered he; "and I will play to you meantime." So when she had crept into the hedge in a great hurry to gather the flower (for she well knew what it was), he began to play upon his flute; and, whether she liked it or not, such was the wonderful power of the music that she was forced to dance a merry jig, on and on without any rest. And as he did not cease playing a moment, the thorns at length tore the clothes from off her body, and pricked her sorely, and there she stuck quite fast.

Then May-bird was free once more; but she was very tired, and Roland said, "Now I will hasten home for help, and by and by

we will be married." And May-bird said,
" I will stay here in the mean time and wait
for you; and, that no one may know me, I
will turn myself into a stone and lie in the
corner of yonder field." Then Roland went
away, and May-bird was to wait for him.
But Roland met with another maiden, who
pleased him so much that he stopped where
she lived, and forgot his former friend; and
when May-bird had staid in the field a long
time, and found he did not come back, she became quite sorrowful, and turned herself into a
little daisy, and thought to herself, " Some one
will come and tread me under foot, and so my
sorrows will end." But it so happened that as
a shepherd was keeping watch in the field he
found the flower, and thinking it very pretty,
took it home, placed it in a box in his
room, and said, " I have never found so
pretty a flower before." From that time every
thing throve wonderfully at the shepherd's
house: when he got up in the morning,
all the household work was ready done;
the room was swept and cleaned; the fire
made, and the water fetched: and in the

afternoon, when he came home, the table-cloth was laid and a good dinner ready set for him. He could not make out how all this happened; for he saw no one in his house : and although it pleased him well enough, he was at length troubled to think how it could be, and went to a cunning woman who lived hard by, and asked her what he should do. She said, " There must be witchcraft in it; look out tomorrow morning early, and see if any thing stirs about in the room; if it does, throw a white cloth at once over it, and then the witchcraft will be stopped." The shepherd did as she said, and the next morning saw the box open and the daisy come out : then he sprang up quickly and threw a white cloth over it : in an instant the spell was broken, and May-bird stood before him ; for it was she who had taken care of his house for him ; and as she was so beautiful he asked her if she would marry him. She said " No," because she wished to be faithful to her dear Roland; but she agreed to stay and keep house for him.

Time passed on, and Roland was to be

married to the maiden that he had found; and according to an old custom in that land, all the maidens were to come and sing songs in praise of the bride and bride-groom. But May-bird was so grieved when she heard that her dearest Roland had forgotten her, and was to be married to another, that her heart seemed as if it would burst within her, and she would not go for a long time. At length she was forced to go with the rest; but she kept hiding herself behind the others until she was left the last. Then she could not any longer help coming forward; and the moment she began to sing, Roland sprang up, and cried out, " That is the true bride ; I will have no other but her ;" for he knew her by the sound of her voice; and all that he had forgotten came back into his mind, and his heart was opened towards her. So faithful May-bird was married to her dear Roland, and there was an end of her sorrows ; and from that time forward she lived happily till she died.

THE MOUSE, THE BIRD, AND THE SAUSAGE.

Once upon a time a mouse, a bird, and a sausage took it into their heads to keep house together: and to be sure they managed to live for a long time very comfortably and happily; and beside that added a great deal to their store, so as to become very rich. It was the bird's business to fly every day into the forest and bring wood; the mouse had to carry the water, to make the fire, and lay the cloth for dinner; but the sausage was cook to the household.

He who is too well off often begins to be lazy and to long for something fresh. Now it happened one day that our bird met with one of his friends, to whom he boasted greatly of his good plight. But the other bird laughed at him for a poor fool, who worked hard, whilst the two at home had an easy job of it: for when the mouse had made her fire and fetched the water, she went and laid down in her own little room

till she was called to lay the cloth ; and the
sausage sat by the pot, and had nothing to
do but to see that the food was well cooked ;
and when it was meal time, had only to butter, salt, and get it ready to eat, which it
could do in a minute. The bird flew home,
and having laid his burden on the ground,
they all sat down to table, and after they had
made their meal slept soundly until the next
morning. Could any life be more glorious
than this ?

The next day the bird, who had been told
what to do by his friend, would not go into
the forest, saying, he had waited on them,
and been made a fool of long enough ; they
should change about, and take their turns at
the work. Although the mouse and the
sausage begged hard that things might go on
as they were, the bird carried the day. So
they cast lots, and the lot fell upon the sausage to fetch wood, while the mouse was to be
cook, and the bird was to bring the water.

What happened by thus taking people from
their proper work ? The sausage set out towards the wood, the little bird made a fire,

the mouse set on the pot, and only waited for the sausage to come home and bring wood for the next day. But the sausage kept away so long that they both thought something must have happened to him, and the bird flew out a little way to look out for him; but not far off he found a dog on the road, who said he had met with a poor little sausage, and taking him for fair prey, had laid hold of him and knocked him down. The bird made a charge against the dog of open robbery and murder; but words were of no use, for the dog said, he found the sausage out of its proper work, and under false colours; and so he was taken for a spy and lost his life. The little bird took up the wood very sorrowfully, and went home and told what he had seen and heard. The mouse and he were very much grieved, but agreed to do their best and keep together.

The little bird undertook to spread the table, and the mouse got ready the dinner; but when she went to dish it up, she fell into the pot and was drowned. When the bird came into the kitchen and wanted the dinner to put upon the table, no cook was to be seen ; so he threw the wood about here, there, and every where, and called and sought on all sides, but still could not find the cook. Meantime the fire fell upon the wood and set it on fire; the bird hastened away to get water, but his bucket fell into the well, and he after it; and so ends the story of this clever family.

THE JUNIPER TREE.

A LONG while ago, perhaps as much as two thousand years, there was a rich man who had a wife of whom he was very fond; but they had no children. Now in the garden before the house where they lived, there stood a juniper tree; and one winter's day as the lady was standing under the juniper tree, paring an apple, she cut her finger, and the drops of blood trickled down upon the snow. " Ah !" said she, sighing deeply and looking down upon the blood, " how happy should I be if I had a little child as white as snow and as red as blood!" And as she was saying this, she grew quite cheerful, and was sure her wish would be fulfilled. And after a little time the snow went away, and soon afterwards the fields began to look green. Next the spring came, and the meadows were dressed with flowers; the trees put forth their green leaves; the young branches shed their blossoms upon the ground; and the little birds sung through the groves. And then came summer, and the sweet-smelling flowers of the juniper tree began to unfold; and the lady's heart leaped within her, and she fell on her knees for joy. But when autumn drew near, the fruit was thick upon the trees. Then the lady plucked the red berries from the juniper tree, and looked sad and sorrowful; and she called her husband to her, and said, " If I die, bury me under the juniper tree." Not long after this a pretty little child was born; it was, as the lady wished, as red as blood, and as white as snow; and as soon as she had looked upon it, her joy overcame her, and she fainted away and died.

Then her husband buried her under the juniper tree, and wept and mourned over her; but after a little while he grew better, and at length dried up his tears, and married another wife.

Time passed on, and he had a daughter born; but the child of his first wife, that was as red as blood, and as white as snow, was a little boy. The mother loved her daughter very much, but hated the little boy, and bethought herself how she might get all her husband's money for her own child; so she used the poor fellow very harshly, and was always pushing him about from one corner of the house to another, and thumping him one while and pinching him another, so that he was for ever in fear of her, and when he came home from school, could never find a place in the house to play in.

Now it happened that once when the mother was going into her store-room, the little girl came up to her, and said, " Mother, may I have an apple?" " Yes, my dear," said she, and gave her a nice rosy apple out of the chest. Now you must know that this

chest had a very thick heavy lid, with a great
sharp iron lock upon it. "Mother," said
the little girl, "pray give me one for my
little brother too." Her mother did not
much like this; however, she said, "Yes,
my child; when he comes from school, he
shall have one too." As she was speaking,
she looked out of the window and saw the
little boy coming; so she took the apple from
her daughter, and threw it back into the
chest and shut the lid, telling her that
she should have it again when her brother
came home. When the little boy came to
the door, this wicked woman said to him with
a kind voice, "Come in, my dear, and I
will give you an apple." "How kind you
are, mother!" said the little boy; "I should
like to have an apple very much." "Well,
come with me then," said she. So she took
him into the store-room and lifted up the
cover of the chest, and said, "There, take
one out yourself;" and then, as the little
boy stooped down to reach one of the apples
out of the chest, bang! she let the lid fall,
so hard that his head fell off amongst the

apples. When she found what she had done, she was very much frightened, and did not know how she should get the blame off her shoulders. However, she went into her bed-room, and took a white handkerchief out of a drawer, and then fitted the little boy's head upon his neck, and tied the handkerchief round it, so that no one could see what had happened, and seated him on a stool before the door with the apple in his hand.

Soon afterwards Margery came into the kitchen to her mother, who was standing by the fire, and stirring about some hot water in a pot. "Mother," said Margery, "my brother is sitting before the door with an apple in his hand; I asked him to give it me, but he did not say a word, and looked so pale, that I was quite frightened." "Nonsense!" said her mother; "go back again, and if he won't answer you, give him a good box on the ear." Margery went back, and said, "Brother, give me that apple." But he answered not a word; so she gave him a box on the ear; and immediately his head fell off. At this, you may be sure she was sadly frightened, and ran screaming out to her mother, that she had knocked off her brother's head, and cried as if her heart would break. "O Margery!" said her mother, "what have you been doing? However, what is done cannot be undone; so we had better put him out of the way, and say nothing to any one about it."

When the father came home to dinner, he said, "Where is my little boy?" And his wife said nothing, but put a large dish of black soup upon the table; and Margery wept bitterly all the time, and could not hold up her head. And the father asked after his little boy again. "Oh!" said his wife, "I should think he is gone to his uncle's." "What business could he have to go away without bidding me good bye?" said his father. "I know he wished very much to go," said the woman; "and begged me to let him stay there some time; he will be well taken care of there." "Ah!" said the father, "I don't like that; he ought not to have gone away without wishing me good-bye." And with that he began to eat; but he seemed

still sorrowful about his son, and said, " Margery, what do you cry so for? your brother
will come back again, I hope." But Margery by and by slipped out of the room
and went to her drawers and took her best
silk handkerchief out of them, and tying it
round her little brother's bones, carried
them out of the house weeping bitterly all
the while, and laid them under the juniper
tree; and as soon as she had done this,
her heart felt lighter, and she left off crying. Then the juniper tree began to move
itself backwards and forwards, and to stretch
its branches out, one from another, and then
bring them together again, just like a person
clapping hands for joy: and after this, a kind
of cloud came from the tree, and in the middle
of the cloud was a burning fire, and out of
the fire came a pretty bird, that flew away
into the air, singing merrily. And as soon as
the bird was gone, the handkerchief and the
little boy were gone too, and the tree looked
just as it had done before; but Margery felt
quite happy and joyful within herself, just as

if she had known that her brother had been alive again, and went into the house and ate her dinner.

But the bird flew away, and perched upon the roof of a goldsmith's house, and sang,

> " My mother slew her little son;
> My father thought me lost and gone:
> But pretty Margery pitied me,
> And laid me under the juniper tree;
> And now I rove so merrily,
> As over the hills and dales I fly:
> O what a fine bird am I!

The goldsmith was sitting in his shop finishing a gold chain; and when he heard the bird singing on the house-top, he started up so suddenly that one of his shoes slipped off; however, without stopping to put it on again, he ran out into the street with his apron on, holding his pincers in one hand, and the gold chain in the other. And when he saw the bird sitting on the roof with the sun shining on its bright feathers, he said, " How sweetly you sing, my pretty bird! pray sing that song again." " No," said the bird, " I can't sing twice for nothing; if you will give me that gold chain, I'll try what I can do." " There," said the goldsmith, " take the chain, only pray sing that song again." So the bird flew down, and taking the chain in its right claw, perched a little nearer to the goldsmith, and sang:

" My mother slew her little son;
    My father thought me lost and gone:
    But pretty Margery pitied me,
    And laid me under the juniper tree;
    And now I rove so merrily,
    As over the hills and dales I fly:
        O what a fine bird am I!

After that the bird flew away to a shoe-maker's, and sitting upon the roof of the house, sang the same song as it had done before.

When the shoemaker heard the song, he ran to the door without his coat, and looked up to the top of the house; but he was obliged to hold his hand before his eyes, because the sun shone so brightly. " Bird," said he, " how sweetly you sing!" Then he called into the house, " Wife! wife! come

out here, and see what a pretty bird is singing on the top of our house!" And he
called out his children and workmen; and
they all ran out and stood gazing at the bird,
with its beautiful red and green feathers,
and the bright golden ring about its neck,
and eyes which glittered like the stars. "O
bird!" said the shoemaker, "pray sing that
song again." "No," said the bird, "I cannot sing twice for nothing; you must give me
something if I do." "Wife," said the shoemaker, "run up stairs into the workshop,
and bring me down the best pair of new red
shoes you can find." So his wife ran and
fetched them. "Here, my pretty bird," said
the shoemaker, "take these shoes; but pray
sing that song again." The bird came down,
and taking the shoes in his left claw, flew up
again to the house-top, and sang:

> "My mother slew her little son;
> My father thought me lost and gone:
> But pretty Margery pitied me,
> And laid me under the juniper tree;
> And now I rove so merrily,
> As over the hills and dales I fly:
> O what a fine bird am I!"

And when he had done singing, he flew away, holding the shoes in one claw and the chain in the other. And he flew a long, long way off, till at last he came to a mill. The mill was going clipper! clapper! clipper! clapper! and in the mill were twenty millers, who were all hard at work hewing a mill-stone; and the millers hewed, hick! hack! hick! hack! and the mill went on, clipper! clapper! clipper! clapper!

So the bird perched upon a linden tree close by the mill, and began its song:

> " My mother slew her little son;
>   My father thought me lost and gone:"

here two of the millers left off their work and listened:

> " But pretty Margery pitied me,
>   And laid me under the juniper tree;"

now all the millers but one looked up and left their work;

> " And now I rove so merrily,
>   As over the hills and dales I fly:
>   O what a fine bird am I!"

Just as the song was ended, the last miller heard it, and started up, and said, "O
bird! how sweetly you sing! do let me hear
the whole of that song; pray, sing it again!"
"No," said the bird, "I cannot sing twice
for nothing; give me that millstone, and I'll
sing again." "Why," said the man, "the
millstone does not belong to me; if it was
all mine, you should have it and welcome."
"Come," said the other millers, "if he will
only sing that song again, he shall have the
millstone." Then the bird came down from
the tree: and the twenty millers fetched long
poles and worked and worked, heave, ho!
heave, ho! till at last they raised the millstone
on its side; and then the bird put its head
through the hole in the middle of it, and flew
away to the linden tree, and sang the same
song as it had done before.

And when he had done, he spread his
wings, and with the chain in one claw, and
the shoes in the other, and the millstone
about his neck, he flew away to his father's
house.

Now it happened that his father and mother and Margery were sitting together at dinner. His father was saying, " How light and cheerful I am ! " But his mother said, " Oh I am so heavy and so sad, I feel just as if a great storm was coming on." And Margery said nothing, but sat and cried. Just then the bird came flying along, and perched upon the top of the house; " Bless me ! " said the father, " how cheerful I am ; I feel as if I was about to see an old friend again." " Alas ! " said the mother, " I am so sad, and my teeth chatter so, and yet it seems as if my blood was all on fire in my veins ! " and she tore open her gown to cool herself. And Margery sat by herself in a corner, with her plate on her lap before her, and wept so bitterly that she cried her plate quite full of tears.

And the bird flew to the top of the juniper tree and sang:

" My mother slew her little son;—"

Then the mother held her ears with her hands, and shut her eyes close, that she might neither see nor hear; but there was a sound in her ears like a frightful storm, and her eyes burned and glared like lightning.

"My father thought me lost and gone:—"

"O wife!" said the father, "what a beautiful bird that is, and how finely he sings; and his feathers glitter in the sun like so many spangles!"

"But pretty Margery pitied me,
And laid me under the juniper tree;—"

At this Margery lifted up her head and sobbed sadly, and her father said, "I must go out, and look at that bird a little nearer." "Oh! don't leave me alone," said his wife; "I feel just as if the house was burning." However, he would go out to look at the bird; and it went on singing:

"But now I rove so merrily,
As over the hills and dales I fly:
O what a fine bird am I!"

As soon as the bird had done singing, he let fall the gold chain upon his father's neck,

and it fitted so nicely that he went back into
the house and said, " Look here, what a
beautiful chain the bird has given me; only
see how grand it is!" But his wife was
so frightened that she fell all along on the
floor, so that her cap flew off, and she lay as
if she were dead. And when the bird began
singing again, Margery said, " I must go
out and see whether the bird has not something to give me." And just as she was going out of the door, the bird let fall the red
shoes before her; and when she had put on
the shoes, she all at once became quite light
and happy, and jumped into the house and
said, " I was so heavy and sad when I went
out, and now I'm so happy! see what fine
shoes the bird has given me!" Then the
mother said, " Well, if the world should
fall to pieces, I must go out and try whether
I shall not be better in the air." And as she
was going out, the bird let fall the mill-stone
upon her head and crushed her to pieces.

The father and Margery hearing the noise
ran out, and saw nothing but smoke and fire

and flame rising up from the place; and when this was passed and gone, there stood the little boy beside them; and he took his father and Margery by the hand, and they went into the house, and ate their dinner together very happily.

NOTES

The Goose Girl, p. 1.—" Die Gänse-magd " of MM.
Grimm ; a story from Zwehrn. In the *Pentamerone*,
iv. 7, there is a story which remarkably agrees with
the present in some of its circumstances. The in-
tended bride is thrown overboard while sailing to her
betrothed husband, and the false one takes her place.
The king is dissatisfied with the latter, and in his pas-
sion sends the brother of the lost lady (who had re-
commended his sister) to keep his geese. The true
bride, who has been saved by a beautiful mermaid, or
sea-nymph, rises from the water, and feeds the geese
with princely food and rose-water. The king watches,
observes the fair lady combing her beautiful locks, from
which pearls and diamonds fall; and the fraud is disco-
vered. The story of the Goose Girl is certainly a very
remarkable one, and has several traits of very original
and highly traditional character. Tacitus mentions the
divination of the ancient Germans by horses. Saxo
Grammaticus also tells how the heads of horses offered
in sacrifices were cut off: and the same practice among
the Wendi is mentioned by Prætorius. The horse without a head is mentioned by the Quarterly Reviewer as
appearing in a Spanish story, and he vouches for its having
also migrated into this country. "A friend," he adds,
"has pointed out a passage in *Plato de Legibus*, lib. vi., in

which the sage alludes to a similar superstition among the Greeks." Where the horse got his name of Falada MM. Grimm profess not to know, though the coincidence of the first syllable inclines them to assign to it some consanguinity with Roland's steed. The golden and silvery hair is often met with in these tales, and the speaking charm given by the mother (which is in the original a drop of blood, not a lock of hair) is also not uncommon.

In the original, an oath is extorted by force from the true bride, and it is that which prevents her disclosure of the story to the king, who finds out a plan for her evading the oath, by telling the tale into the oven's mouth, whence of course it reaches him, though in a sufficiently second-hand way to save the fair lady's conscience.

Faithful John, p. 12.—" Der getreue Johannes ; " from Zwehrn. Another somewhat similar story is current in Paderborn. The tale is a singular one, and contains so much of Orientalism that the reader would almost suppose himself in the *'Arabian Nights' Entertainments.*

In the *Pentamerone,* iv. 9, is a story very much resembling this : the birds who foretell and forewarn against the disasters are two doves ; and the whole happens by the contrivance, and is finally remedied by the power of an enchanter, the lady's father, who had sent the perils that menace the prince, in revenge for the carrying away of his daughter.

It should be added, that in the original, the father really cuts off the heads of his two children, who are restored to life in reward for his faith.

The reader will observe the coincidence of one portion of the story with the Greek fable of the Garment of Dejanira.

The Blue Light, p. 26.—" Das blaue Licht ;" a Mecklenburgh story. In the Collection of Hungarian Tales of Georg von Gaal, it appears that there is one like this, called " The Wonderful Tobacco Pipe."

Ashputtel, p. 33.—" Aschen-puttel." Several versions of this story are current in Hesse and Zwehrn, and it is one of the most universal currency. We understand that it is popular among the Welsh, as it is also among the Poles ; and Schottky found it among the Servian fables. Rollenhagen in his *Froschmäuseler* (a Satire of the sixteenth century,) speaks of the tale of the despised Aschen-pössel ; and Luther illustrates from it the subjection of Abel to his brother Cain. MM. Grimm trace out several other proverbial allusions even in the Scandinavian traditions. And lastly, the story is in the Neapolitan *Pentamerone,* under the title of " Cennerentola." An ancient Danish ballad has the incident of the mother hearing from her grave the sorrows of her child ill-used by the step-mother, and ministering thence to its relief. " The Slipper of Cinderella finds a parallel, though somewhat sobered, in the history of the celebrated Rhodope ;"—so says the Editor of the new edition of Warton, vol. i. (86).

The Young Giant and the Tailor, p. 46.—This is compounded of two of MM. Grimm's tales, " Der junge Riese" and " Das tapfere Schneiderlein," with some curtailments, particularly in the latter. The whole has an intimate connexion with the oldest Northern traditions, and will be recognised as concur-

ring in many of its incidents with the tales of *Owlglass,*
Hickathrift, &c. so well known, and on which a good deal
was said in the notes to the first volume. The service
to the smith is a remarkable coincidence with Siegfried's
adventures ; and the mill-stone that falls harmless, re-
minds us of Thor's adventure with Skrimnir. The
giant, moreover, is in true keeping with the Northern
personages of that description, for whom the shrewd
dwarf is generally more than a match ; and the pranks
played belong to the same class of performances as
those of the hero Grettir when he kept geese upon the
common. MM. Grimm quote a Servian tale given by
Schottky, which resembles closely the conflict of the
wits between the giant and the young man.

See further on the subject of the smith, the remarks of the Editor of the new edition of Warton's
History of English Poetry, in his Preface, p. (89).

The Crows and the Soldier, p. 67.—" Die Krähen ; "
a Mecklenburgh story. MM. Grimm mention a similar tale by the Persian poet Nisami, recently noticed by
Hammer ; and they also notice coincidences in Bohe-
mian and Hungarian tales.

Peewit, p. 74.—Is a translation of a story called
Kibitz, from the *Volks-Sagen, Märchen, und Legenden,*
of J. G. Büsching ; but the tale in almost all its incidents coincides in substance with " Das Bürle " of
MM. Grimm, who give two versions of it. It resembles in some instances the " Scarpafico " of Straparola,
i. 3 ; and also *Pentamerone,* ii. 10 ; as well as an adventure in the English *History of Friar Bacon and his Man.*

Hans and his Wife, p. 82.—This comprises the three

stories of Grimm, "Die kluge Grethel," "Der ge-
scheidte Hans," and "Die faule Spinnerin," which we
have taken the liberty of ascribing to one couple.
The first is taken immediately by MM. Grimm, (though
a story also of popular currency,) from what they
describe to be a rare book, *Ovum Paschale*, Salzburg,
1700. It is also the subject of a Meistergesang in a
MS. in the possession of Arnim, and of one of Hans
Sachs' tales, "Die Vernascht Köchin." The second
resembles two different stories given in books printed
in Germany in 1557 and 1565. "Bardiello," in the *Pentamerone*, i. 4, resembles the story in several particulars. The third is from Zwehrn, and resembles *Pentamerone*, iv.4, as well as an old German tale printed in
the *Altdeutsche Wälder*.

Cherry, or the Frog-Bride, p. 97.—This is a transla-
tion of " Das Märchen von der Padde," from Büsching's
Volks-Sagen; changing the heroine from " Petersilie "
(Parsley) into Cherry.

Mother Holle, p. 108.—The " Frau Holle " of MM.
Grimm : from Hesse and Westphalia, and several other
places, but with variations. It is a common saying in
Hesse, when it snows, " Mother Holle is making her
bed." Mother Holle, or Hulda, is a potent personage
of some repute, exercising her power for the public
good, in rewarding the industrious and well-disposed,
and punishing the slovenly and mischievous. MM.
Grimm have collected some of her traditions in vol. i.
of their *Deutsche Sagen*; and the same will be found in
Prætorius. She seems to be of heathen origin.

The Water of Life, p. 114.—" Das Wasser der

Lebens; " from Hesse, Paderborn, and (with variations) other places. The story has in many particulars
a very Oriental cast. It resembles one of the *Arabian
Nights*; but it is also connected with one of the tales
of Straparola, iv. 3. Another of MM. Grimm's stories,
" De drei Vügelkens," with which it coincides in several
respects, has still more of the Oriental character. The
" Water of Life" is a very ancient tradition, even in
Rabbinical lore. In Conrad of Wurtzburg's *Trojan
War*, (written in the 13th century,) Medea gets the
water from Paradise to renew the youth of Jason's
father.

Peter the Goatherd, p. 126.—Is the " Ziegenhirt " of
Otmar's Collection of the Ancient Tales and Traditions
current in the Hartz. The name of Frederic Barbarossa
is associated with the earliest cultivation of the muses in
Germany. During the Suabian dynasty, (at the head of
which he is to be placed,) arose and flourished the Min-
nesingers, or poets of love, cotemporary with the Trou-
badours, whom they rival in the quantity, and far excel
in the quality, of their compositions. Frederic was a
patron of the minstrel arts ; and it is remarkable that
the Hartz traditions still make him attached to similar
pursuits, and tell how musicians, who have sought the
caverns where he sits entranced, have been richly rewarded by his bounty.

The author of *The Sketch Book* has made use of
this tale as the plot of his " Rip van Winkle." There
are several German traditions and ballads which turn
on the unsuspected lapse of time under enchantment;
and we may remember in connexion with it, the ancient story of the " Seven Sleepers " of the fifth century (*Gibbon*, vi. 32). That tradition was adopted by

Mahomet, and has, as Gibbon observes, been also adopted and adorned by the nations from Bengal to Africa, who profess the Mahometan religion. It was translated into Latin before the end of the sixth century, by the care of Gregory of Tours ; and Paulus Diaconus (*de Gestis Longobardorum*), in the eighth century, places seven sleepers in the North under a rock by the sea shore. The incident has considerable capability of interest and effect ; and it is not wonderful that it should become popular, and form the basis of various traditions. The next step is to animate the period dropt from real life—the parenthesis of existence —with characteristic adventures, as in the succeeding story of " The Elfin Grove ;" and as in " The Dean of Santiago," a Spanish tale from the Conde Lucanor, translated in the *New Monthly Magazine for August* 1824, where several similar stories are referred to.

The Four Clever Brothers, p. 133.—"Die vier kunstreichen Brüder ;" from Paderborn. There is a story exceedingly like this in the *Pentamerone*, v. 7, " Li cinco Figlie;" and in Straparola, vii. 5. In another old German story, a smith arrives at such perfection, as to shoe a fly with a golden shoe and twenty-four nails to each foot. In the Persian *Tuhti Nameh*, there is also a story closely resembling the one before us. In a fabliau, (to which we cannot refer at the moment,) we recollect the thief is so dexterous as to steal off his companion's breeches without his observation.

The Elfin Grove, p. 112.—This is an abridgement of a story in Tieck's *Phantasus*, founded on an old and well known tradition, but considerably amplified by him. We have reduced it nearer to its primitive ele-

ments ; but it is, of course, to a great extent, a fancy
piece, and does not pretend to that authenticity of popular currency which is claimed for the other stories. The
principal incident resembles that in " Peter the Goatherd ;" and more closely, that which has been turned to
so much account by Mr. Hogg, in the *Queen's Wake*.
The song is written by a friend, and has been adapted to
a German popular air.

The Salad, p. 153.—The " Krautesel" of MM.
Grimm. The transformation will of course remind the
reader of *Apuleius*. See also Prætorius, ii. 452, where
the lily has the restorative power. But the whole is
only another version of the story of *Fortunatus*, the
origin of which is not known, though the common version of it was probably got up in Spain, if we may judge
by the names Andalusia, Marsepia, and Ampedo. One
version of it is in the *Gesta Romanorum*.

See some observations on the nature of the precious
gifts, on which the plot of this and the following story
turns, in the preface to the new edition of Warton's
History of English Poetry, p. (66).

The Nose, p. 164.—This story comes from Zwehrn,
and has been given by MM. Grimm only in an abridged
form in their notes ; but we wished to preserve the adventures substantially, as connected with the last story,
and as illustrating the antiquity and general diffusion
of the leading incidents of both. The usual excrescence
is a horn or horns ; not as here, " nasus, qualem no-
luerit ferre rogatus Atlas."

The Five Servants, p. 176.—In MM. Grimm there
are six, but we have omitted one for delicacy's sake.

The story was heard by them in Paderborn. In several other places they found a story agreeing with it in general character, as do also " Lo Gnorante," (Dummling,) in the *Pentamerone*, iii. 8, an Arabian story translated in the *Cabinet des Fées*, tom. xxxix. p. 421 ; and another in the *Gesta Romanorum*.

Catskin, p. 188.—The " Allerlei-rauh " of MM. Grimm ; a Hessian and Paderborn tale. It is known as Perrault's " Peau d' Ane," and as " Ll' orza," of the *Pentamerone*, ii. 6.—See also Straparola, i. 4.

The Robber Bridegroom, p. 199.—" Der Raüberbraütigam " of MM. Grimm. This tale has a general affinity to that of *Bluebeard*, most of the incidents of which story are found in others of the German collection. It should, perhaps, be observed, that in the original, the *finger* is chopped off, and is carried away by the bride, as well as the ring upon it.

The Three Sluggards, p. 205.—The " Drei Faulen," of MM. Grimm, who quote a similar story from the *Gesta Romanorum*.

The Seven Ravens, p. 206.—" Die sieben Raben," of MM. Grimm. This story, wild and incoherent as it is, will perhaps be considered curious, as peculiarly Northern and original in its character and incidents. The " Glasberg," or Glass Mountain at the World's End, receives from MM. Grimm some interesting illustrations.

Roland and Maybird, p. 211.—We must apologize to the reader of the original, for the way in which three stories, viz. " Fundevogel," " Der Liebste Roland,"

and " Hänsel and Grethel," have been here combined
in one. Several of the incidents will be familiar
to the English reader : indeed, they are common
to almost every country, and are found as well in
the Neapolitan *Pentamerone* as in the Hungarian
Collection of Georg von Gaal. We apprehend that the
concluding part of the story is not quite correctly pre-
served ; and that, for the credit of the hero, the maiden
who seduces him from his old attachment, ought to be,
as in " The Lady and the Lion," an enchantress, whose
spell is broken by the sound of the true mistress's
voice. Those who wish to trace the dance-inspiring in-
strument of music, through all its forms of tradition,
must be referred to " the Editor's preface" to the new
edition of Warton, (p. 64.)

The Mouse, the Bird, and the Sausage, p. 226. This
is translated here only as a specimen of the whim-
sical assortments of *dramatis personæ* which the German story tellers have sometimes made.

The Juniper Tree, p. 229.—" Van den Machandel-
Boom " of MM. Grimm. We must acquaint the reader that in the original the black broth which the father
eats, is formed by the step-mother from the limbs
of the murdered child. This incident we thought right
to omit, though it must be noted here as one of the
curious circumstances of coincidence with other traditions. The bones buried by Margery are those which
the father unconsciously picks and throws under the
table. The song in the original is as follows :

> " Min Moder de mi slacht't,
> Min Vader de mi att,
> Min Swester de Marleeniken
> Söcht alle mine Beeniken,

Un bindt se in een syden Dook,
Legts unner den Machandel-boom.
Kywitt! Kywitt! ach watt een schön Vagel bin ick ! ''

A literal translation of which would be,

" My mother me slew;
My father me ate ;
My sister Margery
Gather'd all my bones,
And bound them up in a silken shroud,
And laid them under the juniper tree.
Kywit ! Kywit! ah, what a fine bird am I ! ''

On this story we meant to have added some observations of our own ; but as the Editor of Warton has re-
viewed us by a sort of anticipation, we will with pleasure
content ourselves with a quotation of his remarks, (Preface 87.) "The most interesting tale in the whole collection, whether we speak with reference to its contents, or
the admirable style of the narrative, ' the Machandel-
Boom,' is but a popular view of the same mythos upon
which the Platonists have expended so much commen-
tary—the history of the Cretan Bacchus, or Zagreus.
This extraordinary tale will be found in the second volume of the German Stories, now on the eve of publication. The points of coincidence may be thus briefly stated.
In the Cretan fable, the destruction of Zagreus is attri-
buted to the jealousy of his step-mother Juno ; and the
Titans (those telluric powers who were created to
avenge their mother's connubial wrongs) are the instru-
ments of her cruelty. The infant god is allured to an
inner chamber, by a present of toys and fruit, (among
these an *apple*,) and is forthwith murdered. The dis-
membered body is now placed in a kettle, for the repast
of his destroyers; but the vapour ascending to heaven,

the deed is detected, and the perpetrators struck dead
by the lightning of Jove. Apollo collects the bones of
his deceased brother, and buries them at Delphi, where
the palingenesy of Bacchus was celebrated periodically
by the Hosii and Thyades. (Compare *Clemens Alex.
Protrept.* p. 15. ed. Potter; *Nonnus Dionys.* vi. 174, &c.
and *Plutarch, de Isid. et Osirid.* c. 35. et *De Esu Car-
nium,* i. c. vii.) But this again is only another version
of the Egyptian mythos relative to Osiris, which will
supply us with the chest, the tree, the sisterly affection,
and perhaps the bird (though the last may be explained
on other grounds). (*Plut. de Isid.* &c. c. 13. et seqq.)
Mr. Grimm wishes to consider the ' Machandel-
Boom' the juniper-tree; and not the 'Mandel,' or
almond-tree. It will be remembered, that the latter
was believed by the ancient world to possess very im-
portant properties. The fruit of one species, the
Amygdala, impregnated the daughter of the river San-
garius with the Phrygian Attys (*Paus.* vii. 17); and
another, the Persea, was the sacred plant of Isis, so
conspicuous on Egyptian monuments. (For this inter-
pretation of the Persea, see S. de Sacy's *Abd-allatif, Re-
lation de l'Egypte,* p. 47-72, and the Christian and Ma-
hommedan fictions there cited.) This story of dressing
and eating a child is historically related of Atreus, Tan-
talus, Procne, Harpalice (*Hyginus* ed. Staveren, 206),
and Astyages (*Herod.* i. 119) ; and is obviously a piece
of traditional scandal borrowed from ancient mythology.
The Platonistic exposition of it will be found in Mr. Taylor's tract upon the Bacchic Mysteries, (*Pamphleteer,*
No. 15.)"

The Translator cannot close his work, without congratulating those who have a taste for these subjects, on the publication of the volume which has lately appeared under the title of " Fairy Legends and Traditions of the South of Ireland."—It may be referred to throughout for the curious illustrations which it affords of mutual affinities between the traditionary tales of widely separated nations ; and it will, it is trusted, give rise to similar endeavours to preserve, while it can yet be done, the popular stories of other parts of the British Empire. Cornwall, Wales, the North of England, and Scotland might each afford an interesting addition to the common stock.

THE END.